THE HIDDEN

A Monika Paniatowski Mystery

Sally Spencer

This first world edition published 2017
in Great Britain and the USA by
SEVERN HOUSE PUBLISHERS LTD of
Eardley House, 4 Uxbridge Street, London W8 7SY.
Trade paperback edition first published
in Great Britain and the USA 2018 by
SEVERN HOUSE PUBLISHERS LTD.

British Library Cataloguing in Publication Data
A CIP catalogue record for this title is available from the British Library.

ISBN-13: 978-0-7278-8707-8 (cased)
ISBN-13: 978-1-84751-812-5 (trade paper)
ISBN-13: 978-1-78010-876-6 (e-book)

All Severn House titles are printed on acid-free paper.

Severn House Publishers support the Forest Stewardship Council™ [FSC™],
the leading international forest certification organisation.
All our titles that are printed on FSC certified paper carry the FSC logo.

MIX
Paper from
responsible sources
FSC
www.fsc.org   FSC® C013056

Typeset by Palimpsest Book Production Ltd.,
Falkirk, Stirlingshire, Scotland.
Printed and bound in Great Britain by
TJ International, Padstow, Cornwall.

To Ava

PROLOGUE

I t was by the purest of pure chance that Millicent and Janice Knightly – PC Michael Knightly's two young daughters – discovered the body in the grounds of Stamford Hall.

Mike Knightly's original intention, on that Sunday in June, had been to drive up to the Lake District. Then, while he was having his breakfast cereal, he heard the weatherman on the radio announce that it was expected to rain buckets over Lake Windermere, and that was enough to convince him that it might be wise to come up with a plan B.

'You know how thoroughly miserable both the kids get when it's wet,' he said to his wife, Ginny, 'so why don't we forget the lakes and go to Stamford Hall, instead?'

'Stamford Hall? Wasn't there a murder there – or am I thinking of somewhere else?' Ginny Knightly asked.

'No, it was there all right – the victim was a reporter from a national newspaper, I think – but that must have been well over two years ago,' said Knightly, doing his best to avoid the need to come up with a plan C.

'Oh, it was over two years ago, was it?' his wife countered. 'Well, that's all right then – if it was *over two years ago*, it must be the perfect spot to take the kids. I mean, it's not as if there's likely to be a nasty atmosphere about the place, now, is there. Mike?'

There were times when Knightly really appreciated his wife's slightly sarcastic sense of humour – but this was not one of them.

'There've been a lot of changes made to Stamford Hall since the murder,' he protested.

And so there had been. Since the murder, the estate's owner, the 13th Earl of Ridley, had gone (rumour had it he'd been detained under the Mental Health Act) and he'd been replaced by a distant cousin, who had immediately begun turning the Hall into a popular tourist attraction.

Ginny thought about it for a second – considering, among other factors, the possibility that one of the changes might have been the introduction of craft and souvenir shops – then said, 'I suppose we could give it a try. If you can believe the weather forecast, at least we won't get rained on there.'

From the start, the expedition to Stamford Hall was judged a success by everyone involved in it.

The weather was gorgeous, and the kids were overawed by the very size of the place.

'*How big is it, Daddy?*'

'*Twelve hundred acres.*'

'*Gosh, that is big! What's an acre?*'

They loved the modest zoo – especially the petting section, where there were the sweetest goats. They relished their fish and chip lunch (mushy peas five pence extra, but well worth it), which they ate at the cafe overlooking the boating lake. After lunch, they hired a boat on the lake – the exercise would get rid of all those calories, Knightly told himself – then went to the fairground, where the girls embraced the opportunity of being spun giddy and sick.

And finally, as teatime approached, they drove to the Backend Woods picnic area, which was about two miles from the West Gate. The picnic area had a large car park, and from the evidence of the full-to-overflowing rubbish bins, had been heavily used earlier in the day, but now, at almost five o'clock, there was only one other vehicle – a Ford Cortina – parked there.

Sitting at one of the stone tables, they ate their corned beef sandwiches and hard-boiled eggs with gusto. The girls drank orange cordial, the adults sipped tea from a tartan flask.

When they'd finished eating, Knightly lit up a cigarette.

'Well, this has been a grand day, hasn't it?' he said – more to himself than anyone else.

'Can me and Millie go and play hide and seek in the woods, Daddy?' Janice asked.

Knightly glanced down at his watch. 'All right,' he said, 'but I don't want you going too far.'

'And come back every few minutes, so we know you're all right,' Ginny added.

'Have *you* enjoyed yourself, love?' Knightly asked his wife.

'I have,' Ginny replied. 'It's been one of them days when you don't entirely regret not strangling your children at birth.'

Knightly chuckled, and took another drag on his cigarette. And then he saw Janice, red-faced and gasping for breath, suddenly emerging from the woods.

'What's the matter, love?' he asked, alarmed.

'Daddy, Daddy, come and see, there's a lady in there lying down!' Janice shouted.

Knightly relaxed, and did his best to hide the smile which had inevitably come to his face.

'And did this lady have a gentleman with her, lying down next to her?' he asked.

'No!' Janice screamed, furious at not being taken seriously. 'There wasn't a man – and there was blood all round her head.'

Knightly jumped to his feet, and rushed across to where his daughter was standing.

'Where's our Millie, Janice?' he asked, crouching down so that his eyes were level with hers, and placing his large hands on her small thin shoulders. 'Where is she?' he demanded, perhaps shaking her harder than he'd intended.

'I'm here, Daddy,' he heard a voice say from just behind him.

He stood up and turned around, just as Ginny arrived on the scene and swept Millie up into her arms.

'Where's this lady, Janice?' Knightly asked. 'Tell me exactly where you found her.'

'She's . . . she's down that path there,' Janice said, pointing, shakily at a rough track.

'Look after these two,' Knightly told his wife over his shoulder, as he jogged down the path, mostly dodging the branches of trees which overhung it.

'Mike, you're never going to just run off and leave—!' he heard his wife bellow.

But he wasn't going to stop to hear the rest, because he was as certain as he could be that his family didn't need his protection – and a bobby was never really off duty.

It was as the path veered slightly to the right that he saw her. She was lying parallel to the path, between two ancient oaks, and was wearing a pale blouse and a light brown skirt.

Her hair was quite long, blonde and curly, and she looked vaguely familiar to him.

She had very good legs (oh God, how could he be thinking of

that *now*? he asked himself in self-disgust), but they were not *young* legs – the legs of a teenager – and he would probably put her age at somewhere between the mid-thirties and the mid-forties.

When he drew level with the supine woman, he came to a halt, took a couple of deep measured breaths to calm himself down, and then knelt carefully down next to her.

Janice had been right, he thought – the woman must have lost a lot of blood – and it had stained the ground a deep brown as it formed its obscene aura around her head.

He reached out to feel for the pulse in her neck, and got his first real look at her face.

'Jesus, I know you,' he told the woman. 'I bloody know you! You're DCI Paniatowski!'

ONE

The west gate of Stamford Hall was (like the gates in the centres of the other three boundary walls), an impressive piece of work. Constructed by skilled ironworkers over two centuries earlier, it served as both a formidable barrier and a fine example of early industrial art. It was possible to open both sides of the gate – indeed, the grand carriages of the past had required it – but to make it easier to filter and check the traffic as it left the park, the uniformed sergeant and his team had only opened the left side, and when the big black Wolseley arrived, there was already a queue of twenty-five or thirty vehicles waiting to leave.

The sergeant opened the right-hand gate, and though he could not see the man in the back of the Wolseley through the darkened glass, he saluted smartly. Once the big black car was inside – and much to the annoyance of all those waiting to leave – he closed the right-hand gate again.

Chief Constable Ronald Pickering, sitting in the back of the Wolseley, had been far too distracted to notice the sergeant's show of respect.

Things didn't look good, he told himself, as his driver turned left and followed the boundary road which led to the Backend Woods picnic area – they didn't look good at all.

The problem was, he was only *acting* chief constable (and likely to remain so until George Baxter either went mad enough to be certified or grew sane enough to resign), and *acting* chief constables were perpetually auditioning for the job they were already doing. So every new crisis was a test – a yardstick against which he could be measured – and it was more than possible that losing one of his senior officers might be regarded by those people who mattered as being rather careless.

A roadblock had been set up about a mile and a half from the gate, and it was beyond the roadblock that there was evidence that a serious criminal investigation was already underway.

The acting chief constable quickly scanned the scene.

There were half a dozen patrol cars there, and the men who'd arrived in them were employed in taping off the whole area.

There was an ambulance there, too, and the Land Rover which belonged to Dr Shastri, the police surgeon, so it was a safe bet that Monika Paniatowski hadn't been moved yet.

'Stop right here, constable!' Pickering told his driver, and the driver brought the Wolseley to a halt close to where a square-built muscular man in his thirties was standing.

Pickering got out of the car and walked over to the man.

'Bloody terrible thing to have happened, Colin,' he said, placing a comforting hand on DI Beresford's shoulder.

Beresford – clearly red-eyed – only nodded, as if putting what he was feeling into words would have been just too much.

'Have you any idea what Monika was doing in the woods?' Pickering asked. 'Was it part of an ongoing investigation, do you know?'

And then a new thought occurred to him – one so ghastly that he almost fainted.

'She . . . she didn't have any of her children with her, did she?' he said tremulously.

Because if her kids – her bloody infant twins – had gone missing, there'd be such a stink that he might as well hand in his resignation then and there!

'No, the children weren't with her,' Beresford replied. 'The twins are at home with Elena, the housekeeper, and Louisa has gone over to Yorkshire with her school, to play in a hockey match.'

'Thank God,' Pickering said. 'Now what we need to do is find out why DCI Paniatowski was—'

'She's still breathing,' Beresford interrupted him cuttingly, and with an edge of contempt just discernible in his voice. 'She can't say anything, and I'm not even sure she knows where she is, but she's still breathing – and that's something.'

'Yes, I suppose—'

'I'd have been with her myself, but I didn't want to get in the way of the doc and the paramedics.' Beresford paused. 'Anyway, I thought you might like to know that,' he continued, most of his anger now dissipated.

'Yes . . . yes, of course,' Pickering said awkwardly. 'That should have been the first thing I asked, shouldn't it?'

'Well, it certainly was the first thing *I* asked,' Beresford admitted.

'At any rate, while I'm sure we're all praying she makes a full recovery, we're not medical men, are we, and the only thing *we* can do for Monika ourselves is to try our damnedest to catch the bastard who attacked her!' Pickering said briskly. He looked Beresford straight in the eye. 'I'm right about that, aren't I, Colin?' he challenged.

'Yes, sir, you are right,' Beresford agreed, though any feeling that they might be comrades-in-arms was undercut by the deadpan voice in which he delivered the words.

'So what have you done – in practical detecting terms – so far?' Pickering asked.

'As you can see, we've almost finished sectioning off this area,' Beresford said.

'Yes, yes, but what about the rest of the grounds – the funfair and the zoo? I saw a stream of cars leaving as I arrived. I assume everyone in them has already been questioned, have they?'

'No, sir,' Beresford replied. 'Most of them probably don't even know there's been an attack, but I've made sure the officers on the gate are taking their names and addresses, and—'

'Why didn't you question them first?' Pickering demanded.

'We don't have the manpower.'

'Then you should have waited until sufficient manpower arrived, for God's sake!'

'The gatekeeper tells me he's sold over eight hundred car tickets today,' Beresford said. 'If there were, on average, four people in each car, we're talking about over three thousand folk who need to be interviewed. Add to that the people who arrived on the courtesy buses from the railway station, and we're up to maybe three thousand six hundred. Then there are the ones who came on charter coaches. Even if we'd had the whole force on duty, which, this being a Sunday at the start of the summer leave season—'

'All right, all right, I get the point,' Pickering said. 'Christ, what a mess.' He looked around him, as if searching for inspiration. 'I want you to hold the fort until DCI Dixon gets here,' he said finally.

'Yes, sir.'

'Are the rest of DCI Paniatowski's team here?' he asked.

'Yes, sir.'

Of course they bloody were! Paniatowski's team had a reputation for being so thick with one another that it was said around police headquarters that if you kicked one of them, they all limped.

'Right, you have my permission to stay here as well – for the moment – but the second DCI Dixon arrives with his team, I want you all out of here.'

'We'd prefer to stay, sir,' Beresford said.

'Yes, I'm sure you would, Colin,' Pickering agreed. 'I'm sure you would. But you see, I simply can't allow that. You're far too close to this particular investigation to play any continued active part in it.'

'With respect, sir, it's because we're close to DCI Paniatowski – because we know the way she thinks and what motivates her – that we're essential to the investigation.'

'Your comments have been noted, but the decision has been taken,' Pickering said.

'If we can't investigate it as police officers, then we'll investigate as private citizens,' Beresford said firmly.

'Come on, Colin, be realistic – you can't *be* police officers and private citizens at the same time,' Pickering pointed out.

'I agree,' Beresford said, 'and that's why, if I'm kicked off the investigation, you'll have my resignation on your desk by the end of the day.'

'Don't be ridiculous, you'd never consider—'

'And it won't be the only one – you'll have DS Meadows's and DC Crane's resignations as well.'

'Anyone else? Will the station cat be resigning?'

'No, sir – just me, Meadows and Crane.'

Pickering sighed. 'If you're going to threaten me, DI Beresford, you should at least make sure that your threat is credible,' he said, with a new, harder edge to his voice.

'With respect, sir, it's not a threat, sir – it's a statement of fact,' Beresford said levelly.

Pickering sighed with exasperation. 'Look, I know you're upset, and I'm making allowances for that, but I really can't have you talking to me in this way. Whatever you might say now, you know, deep down inside yourself, that you'd never throw away your career like that – and if you wouldn't, then I'm bloody certain the other two wouldn't.'

Beresford looked around him, and found that the woman he was looking for was stretching yellow police tape between two elm trees.

'Could you come here, Sergeant Meadows?' he called out.

Pickering watched Meadows walk towards them. The sergeant was an enigma to him, and – he suspected – to many other men on the force. She wasn't particularly tall, and she certainly wasn't particularly curvaceous. Her dark hair was cut so short it lay on her head like a piece of black velvet. She rarely smiled, and – even at Christmas parties – never said anything even mildly flirtatious, and yet though he was at the top of the tree, and she was somewhere near the bottom, she sometimes scared him. But even so . . . even so, she featured heavily in his daytime fantasies, and even more often in the darker ones he had when he was asleep.

Meadows came to a halt next to Beresford. 'Is there something I can do for you, sir?' she asked.

'No,' Beresford told her, 'I just want to keep you up to date with the latest developments.' He paused. 'Mr Pickering wants us off this investigation. What do you think of that?'

Meadows shrugged indifferently. 'It's not really my place to think about it at all, is it, sir?' she asked. 'Who is or isn't on the case is entirely the chief constable's decision.'

'Well, at least one of you seems to be capable of looking at things sensibly,' Pickering said, doing his best to keep a complacent smile from curling the edges of his mouth.

'You wouldn't argue, but what would you *do* if you were taken off the case?' Beresford asked Meadows.

'What would I do?' Meadows asked. 'I'd resign, so I could carry out my own investigation. I expect DC Crane would do the same.'

'Clear the way,' a voice shouted. 'Clear the way. There's a stretcher coming through.'

All heads turned towards the woods, as the paramedics appeared, carrying the stretcher between them. By the side of the stretcher, holding a drip high in the air, was Dr Shastri, her usually lively face about as animated as a dried raisin.

And lying strapped onto the stretcher – her head swathed in bandages, her skin the colour of the whitest chalk – was Monika Paniatowski.

Oh Christ, what if she never comes out of it? Beresford thought. What if she stays like this forever?

The paramedics slid the stretcher into the back of the ambulance, then one climbed inside, and the other closed the doors. The engine was already running, and the moment the driver was behind the wheel, the ambulance started to gently pull away.

Beresford turned to the chief constable.

'She's our boss, sir,' he said – and Pickering noticed the moisture forming in his eyes. 'We don't want to make things difficult for you, but we have to be part of the search for Monika's attacker – we don't have any choice.'

If they all resigned, the chief constable thought, it would look as if he hadn't been able to handle them properly – and that would be very bad indeed, especially if the press somehow managed to pick up on it.

'In the light of your obvious strength of feeling, I'm prepared to bend a little more than I normally would,' he said. 'I'll assign you to DCI Dixon's team, if that's what you want.'

He paused, to give them time to respond.

'Thank you, sir,' Meadows said.

'Appreciate it, sir,' Beresford added.

'But I will only do that on the understanding that you do exactly what DCI Dixon tells you he wants you to do,' Pickering said. 'That – and no more. Do you think you'll be able to work within those restrictions?'

'Yes, sir,' Beresford said.

'Of course, sir,' Meadows agreed.

And none of them believed a word of it.

'Somebody's got to be there at Monika's house to deal with Louisa, when she gets back from her match in Yorkshire,' Kate Meadows said, when the chief constable had left.

'I know,' Beresford agreed gloomily. 'I think it had better be me, because I've known her since she was a baby. She calls me Uncle Colin, you know . . .'

'Yes, I've heard her.'

'And I'm almost a member of the family.'

'There's no *almost* about it,' Meadows told him, 'but somebody also has to stay here to make sure we don't get shafted by Rhino

Dixon's band of merry men, and since you're the ranking officer from our side, I think it should be you – which means that I get to break Louisa's heart.'

Was that the real reason she thought she should go and he should stay? Beresford wondered.

Or was it that she thought that big flat-footed Colin Beresford couldn't possibly handle Louisa with the sensitivity the situation would require?

And if it was the latter, should he be offended or relieved?

It was all so confusing – but you were bound to be confused when you'd just seen your best mate being carried away on a stretcher.

'Thanks, Kate,' he said, though he almost never called her by her first name. 'I really appreciate it.'

Meadows shrugged. 'You do what you have to do.'

'Do you have any idea what the boss was doing in the woods this afternoon?' he asked.

Meadows blinked.

'No,' she said.

'Are you sure?' Beresford persisted. 'If we knew *why* she was here, we might have some idea why she was attacked.'

'Whoever attacked her, it had nothing to do with the reason she was here,' Meadows said.

'So you *do* know why she was here!'

'I'd better be going,' Meadows said. 'We don't want Louisa to learn what's happened to her mother from someone else, do we?'

TWO

A convoy of three cars, headed by a mid-range Mercedes-Benz, announced the arrival at the woodland crime scene of Detective Chief Inspector William 'Rhino' Dixon and his team.

The cars came to a halt on the road – just beyond the outer limits of the police tape – and their occupants spilled out onto the tarmac.

Even from a distance, Dixon – who stood six feet four in his stockinged feet, and was as broad as a barn – stuck out from the rest of his team.

He was not the most attractive of men, thought Beresford, watching developments from the edge of the woods. His eyes were small, his nose huge, his thick neck was inclined to lean forward under the weight of his massive head, and his skin was an unhealthy grey. When he spoke, it was with a rasping voice which came from having been a dedicated chain smoker (whenever finances permitted) since the day he put childish things behind him and graduated from the infants' school into the primary.

He had a habit of jabbing whoever he was addressing with a heavily nicotine-stained forefinger, and was reputed to be a bit of a bastard to those officers working for him.

'Still an' all,' other bobbies in the canteen would say, 'he does get results.'

Indeed he did get results, Beresford thought – but they weren't as good as Monika's.

Dixon's team gathered around their boss like adoring school-children around a particularly popular teacher at sports day.

Or perhaps, Beresford thought, they were more like medieval courtiers, who were well aware that their positions in court were entirely dependent on their monarch's approval.

He groaned inwardly.

Medieval courtiers?

Had he actually used 'medieval courtiers' in a comparison with the Mid Lancs police?

He was definitely going to have to give up listening to young Jack Crane so much!

Dixon had begun to address his team. His voice, though scratchy, was quite loud, and the fact that his words were being lifted by the breeze meant that Beresford caught most of them.

'Sergeant Higgins, I want a recent picture of DCI Paniatowski on the front page of every local and regional newspaper within a fifty mile radius of Whitebridge,' Dixon said. 'The newspapers themselves will probably have plenty of photographs of Paniatowski in their own archives – but don't leave the choice to them, select the one you think is likely to be most effective. Got that?'

'Got it, sir.'

'Inspector Marsden, you're in charge of supervising the search of the woods. And bear in mind that when I say I want it searching, I mean I want it *searching* – just get this clear: I want each and every bloody leaf on each and every bloody tree examined as if it – and it *alone* – held the vital clue to the attacker; I want every blade of grass studied as if was a precious antique. And when your lads have been over it all once, I want them to go over it again. Understood?'

'Understood, sir.'

'Right, then bloody well get on with it,' Dixon said.

As his team got to work, DCI Dixon looked around him – and seeming to see Beresford standing there for the first time, waved, as if he were on a day trip and had just spotted a mate.

Beresford – who was convinced that Dixon had *actually* noticed him the moment he'd climbed out of his car – wondered if he should wave back, and decided it might be safer just to walk towards the chief inspector, especially since the chief inspector had begun to walk towards him.

Almost as if Dixon had choreographed it – and maybe he had – they met at the yellow tape.

'I can remember the days when police barriers were made out of cast iron and solid wood,' the chief inspector said. 'Bloody big heavy things, so it's hardly surprising that half the fellers I trained with got hernias and left the force on invalidity pensions. Still, I suppose it was as good a way of sorting the wimps from the men as any – it was certainly a lot better than the personality tests the police trick cyclists are always on at us to take these days.'

Beresford said nothing – as with the wave, he was not sure that a response was either required or expected.

'OK, Shagger, you can relax now that the US Cavalry's here to take over,' Dixon said.

Beresford blinked. He knew his nickname around police head-quarters was Shagger – and as a man who had not lost his virginity until he was thirty, and had been making up for it ever since, he fairly revelled in the name – but no one had ever used it to his face before.

'So how are you bearing up?' Dixon asked.

'Not too well, sir,' the inspector admitted.

'I thought you might say that,' Dixon told him, stepping under the tape. 'Walk with me.'

Rhino set off, taking huge strides, around the edge of the woods. Beresford fell in beside him.

'Any idea what your boss was doing in the woods on a Sunday afternoon, when any sensible person would be at home watching the box and having a good old farting session?' Dixon asked.

'No, sir,' Beresford replied.

But Meadows knows, he thought – and Meadows is refusing, point-blank, to tell me.

'The chief constable would like your team to be grafted onto my team,' Dixon said. 'In fact, it's a little bit more than just liking it – he's bloody insisting on it. Now, why would he want to do something which goes against both established procedure and common sense?'

'Perhaps he thought about it and decided that we'd be useful to you,' Beresford suggested.

'Maybe he did, but if it was just that, he would have dropped it when I said I wasn't interested,' Dixon mused. 'So it has to be more than his own puny thoughts – it has to be something you said.' He grinned unpleasantly. 'What did you do, Shagger – play the resignation card?'

Beresford hesitated for a second, then realized that lying would be a pointless exercise, and nodded his head.

'Silly bugger,' Dixon said, contemptuously.

'Now look, sir, you may not particularly like it, but I felt very strongly that—' Beresford began hotly.

'I'm sure you did,' Dixon interrupted him, 'but, you see, I haven't finished chatting yet.'

'Sorry, sir,' Beresford replied contritely.

'When I said "silly bugger" I wasn't talking about you, Shagger,' DCI Dixon continued. 'I meant him – Chief Constable Pick-your-words-very-carefully. And the reason I called him a silly bugger is because a man in his position can't afford to cave in to pressure from one of his underlings. If you'd made that sort of threat to me, my boot would have been so far up your arse that you'd have *flown* down to that unemployment office.'

I can believe that, Beresford thought.

'But what's been done can't be undone, so let's examine the

situation that we actually find ourselves in,' Dixon suggested. 'I don't want you on my team, mainly because my *lads* don't want you on my team. And the reason *they* don't want you is because this is the kind of investigation in which reputations are made – and they're terrified of outsiders stealing all the glory, especially when the outsiders in question are notorious for doing just that.' He paused. 'Anything you'd like to say, Shagger?'

Plenty, Beresford thought. If we're successful, it's not because we've stolen the work done by other teams – if any of us even tried that, the boss would get rid of him in a heartbeat. No, we're successful because we're all bloody good and the boss is bloody marvellous.

'Well, *is there* anything you'd like to say, Shagger?' Dixon asked.

'Not at the moment, sir.'

'Then you're smarter than most people give you credit for. Now, you do want to be on the team – fairly desperately, if I'm any judge – because you worked for Monika Paniatowski—'

'I *still* work for her,' Beresford interrupted.

'Aye, I suppose it's always as well to look on the bright side of things,' Dixon said. 'The point is, you feel entitled to be involved in the investigation, and I'm not entirely sure that you're wrong.'

'It's not just me,' Beresford said. 'It's Meadows and Crane as well. We all owe Monika a lot.'

'So here's what we're going to do,' Dixon continued. 'You'll attend all the briefings, and anything you feel you have to contribute, you will contribute. In addition, your sergeant can shadow my sergeant. But beyond that, you'll follow your own line of investigation, quite independent of what my team is doing.'

'Thank you, sir,' Beresford said gratefully.

'I haven't finished yet,' Dixon cautioned him. 'See that tree over there?' he continued, pointing to an ancient oak.

'Yes, sir.'

'Go and stand with your back to it, will you?'

'I don't see why I—'

'I'm an old man – humour me,' Dixon said, deceptively coaxingly.

Beresford did as he'd been instructed.

'Now spread your arms out,' Dixon said.

'I'm still not quite sure I—'

'Just do it!'

Beresford did. It was a wide trunk, so even with his arms outstretched, the backs of his hands were still in contact with the rough bark.

'That's just perfect,' Dixon said.

'What is? The tree?' Beresford asked, mystified.

'Yes.'

'Perfect for what?'

'I'll tell you for what,' Dixon said, standing directly in front of him, so that the inspector was forced to stay exactly where he was. 'If your investigation impedes my investigation in any way—' stab, stab, went the chief inspector's nicotine-stained index finger into Beresford's shoulder – 'or if I find you've been holding back information because you want to make the collar yourself—'

'That won't happen,' Beresford promised.

'. . . then I'll bloody crucify you,' Dixon said, jabbing him once more for good measure, 'and this is the very bloody tree I'll crucify you *against*.'

The room, it had to be said, was pleasantly furnished. The chairs were made of light wood, the coffee tables of black, smoked glass. The walls were painted in a soothing blue, and several prints – some of them pastoral scenes, others seascapes – had been mounted on them. There was a public address system – though only an expert like Meadows would have noticed it – but it had made no sound in all the time the two of them had been there, so perhaps some thoughtful person, realizing how painful it might be to those in distress, had decided to disconnect it.

And yet, in all probability, this care and attention had little effect, because everyone and anyone who sat in this room knew – with a terrifying certainty – that beyond the door set in one of the soothingly painted walls, there were people who were dying.

Meadows risked a glance at Louisa Paniatowski. Louisa had her birth mother's dark Mediterranean beauty, but she also had a courage and determination she had acquired from her adoptive mother, the sergeant thought.

The girl had not cried when she'd been told what had happened to the woman who was at the centre of her life, and she was not crying now – but the pain that was emanating from her was almost suffocating.

What are you thinking, Louisa? Meadows wondered. What's going through your brain? Are you imagining what's going on beyond that door?

But Louisa wasn't thinking about that at all – for though her body was in the waiting room, her mind was back in the living room of the Paniatowski family home, some eight hours earlier.

Louisa is sitting at the breakfast table, trying to focus on the hockey match which will take place just across the Lancashire-Yorkshire border – and hence, by definition, in hostile territory – later in the day.

The Yorkshire County Youth team are, she has discovered from her careful research, on average eleven months older than the Lancashire team, which means (the chances are) that they will be just that little bit taller and just that little bit stronger. What the Lancashire captain (Louisa Concepción Paniatowski) needs to do, therefore, is develop a game plan in which strategy and cunning can serve as winning substitutes for physical strength.

But the problem is that every time she makes a serious effort to devise such a plan, her mind quickly drifts back to the buff envelope which arrived in the post the day before, and which – though she knows she should have done it already – she has yet to discuss with her mother.

The envelope contains a letter from the University of Cambridge, and that letter carries a message which Louisa considers to be very bad news indeed – and which will lead to her disappointing her mother deeply.

'I'm sorry, Mum,' she says softly, before attempting to force down some of the breakfast fuel she knows she will need to energize her during the battle with the fierce tribe of Yorkshire women. 'I'm really sorry.'

It is five long – agonizing – minutes before Monika, who has been playing with the twins, finally enters the room.

Louisa waits until she has poured herself a cup of tea, and then says, 'I've heard from Cambridge, Mum.'

Monika reads her face, then reaches across the table and takes her daughter's hand.

'I'm so sorry, my love,' she says, 'but you tried your best, and we always knew it was going to be very difficult.'

Yes, I really did try my best, Louisa thinks – and maybe that was my big mistake.

'I got in,' she says. 'Peterhouse wants me.'

For a moment, Paniatowski considers rebuking her daughter for teasing her, because she's always taught Louisa that teasing shows a lack of respect – but she doesn't want to spoil Louisa's moment of triumph by introducing a jarring note, and so she just says, 'That's wonderful, darling.'

'Peterhouse wants me – but I don't want Peterhouse,' Louisa says.

'If you'd prefer some other Cambridge college, then maybe we could put it off for a year and—'

'I don't want to go to Cambridge at all.'

'Then why did you apply?' Paniatowski asks – and she is almost shouting now.

'Because that was what you wanted me to do!' Louisa counters – and she is almost shouting, too.

'Do you know how many girls would give their eye teeth for a place in Cambridge?' Paniatowski demands.

'I'm sure there must be thousands of them – maybe even millions,' Louisa says. 'But I'm not one of them – I want to be a police cadet, and you know that's what I want!'

'I could have your application rejected, you know,' Paniatowski says. 'I could do it easily.'

'And you would, wouldn't you?' Louisa asks bitterly, 'because it's not about what I want at all, is it – it's all about what you want!'

'That's a terrible thing to say,' Paniatowski answers, her voice suddenly much quieter, her tone almost a tremble. 'I would never . . .'

There is the sound of a motor horn outside.

'That's my coach,' Louisa says, standing up from the table.

'But you can't just leave like that,' Paniatowski protests.

'So what do you want me to do instead?' Louisa asks, in the maddeningly logical adult voice that she sometimes employs. 'Would you like me to tell the driver, four teachers and twenty-seven pupils, that I can't leave yet, because I'm having a bloody row with my mother?'

'We're not having a bloody row,' Paniatowski says – but she recognizes, even as she's speaking, that that is exactly what they're having.

Louisa crosses the room to the corner where she's left her kitbag and hockey stick.

'We'll talk about it when I get home,' she says.

'I had a terrible row with Mum this morning, Kate,' Louisa said, the words gushing from her mouth, like a confession extracted under torture. 'We never – ever – row, but we did this morning, and before we could make it right with each other, I left the house.'

'The reason you left was because you had a hockey match, wasn't it?' Meadows asked.

'Yes, but—'

'Did you win?'

'Does that matter?' Louisa said, in a tone pitched halfway between surprise and outrage.

'Yes, it matters,' Meadows said, with a sudden intensity which quite frightened Louisa. 'Life's hard – and anybody who claims that it *isn't* hard is a bloody liar. It's nothing but a series of defeats and disappointments, from the cradle to the grave – so when you're lucky enough to have a victory, you'd better learn to treasure it. So let me ask you again – did you win?'

'Yes, we won,' Louisa admitted.

'Tell me you feel good about it,' Meadows said.

'I feel good about it,' Louisa said dully.

'Tell me again – and this time, make it sound as if you mean it,' Meadows ordered her.

'I feel good about it,' Louisa repeated and by now she was starting to think that yes, she did.

The door to the intensive care unit opened, and a doctor in her thirties emerged.

'Miss Paniatowski?' she asked.

Louisa nodded.

'How old are you?' the doctor asked.

'Nearly eighteen.'

The doctor frowned, as if that were certainly the wrong answer from her point of view.

'And is the lady with you a relative?' she asked.

'Yes, I am,' Meadows said hurriedly, before Louisa had the chance to spoil things by being honest. 'I'm her Aunt Catherine.'

The doctor cleared her throat. 'We've taken the appropriate action to stop your mother's internal bleeding,' she said. 'We consider more surgery to be neither necessary nor appropriate.'

'So she's going to be all right,' Louisa said with huge relief.

The doctor looked at Meadows for guidance, and Meadows flashed back that Louisa would want to hear the truth, however painful that might be.

'Your mother is in a coma at the moment,' she said. 'We don't know when she'll come out of it. It could be soon, but there's also a chance that it might never happen.'

'Do you . . . do you mean she could stay in a coma for ever?'

'Unfortunately, yes, that's exactly what I mean. It's also possible that she could die tomorrow. You can never tell with cases like hers.'

'But if she *does* come out of the coma, she'll be fine,' Louisa pleaded, clutching at whatever straws she could find floating past her.

'She could have no more than a bad headache,' the doctor said cautiously, 'but it's also possible that her brain might not be all that it was.'

'And what does that mean, exactly?' Louisa asked, resolutely.

'At best, she might just be a little absent-minded. At worst, she'll never be able to take care of herself again.'

'Can I see her?' Louisa asked.

'Of course.'

'And can I spend the night with her?'

'I wouldn't recommend it. A girl of your age needs her sleep.'

'Are you saying I can't?' Louisa demanded.

'No, I'm not saying that,' the doctor admitted.

'I need a few things from home, Kate,' Louisa said. 'Will you drive me there?'

'Sure,' Meadows agreed.

THREE

There was no brass plaque screwed to the corner table in the public bar of the Drum and Monkey to commemorate what had gone on there. There was not even a cardboard reserved sign in the centre of the table. Yet the pub's regular drinkers felt a certain protectiveness towards it. They would never even think of sitting at the table themselves, and would soon warn off any newcomers who felt inclined to park their arses there.

The table served as the spiritual home of Monika Paniatowski's inner team, and had performed the same function for Charlie Woodend's team before it. At this table, ideas had been tossed around across the tops of pints of bitter, and cases been cracked to the sound of salt and vinegar crisps being crunched. So it was unthinkable that when they were involved in a serious investigation, the team would meet anywhere else.

Yet that night, the unthinkable was happening, and the regulars found themselves gazing at the table and wondering why – now the team really needed to get their heads together – it was still empty.

Kate Meadows's approach to driving had once been described as being like a kamikaze pilot high on LSD, but on the way back to the Paniatowski home, she was more like a little old lady paying her weekly visit to church.

'I'm not saying that you shouldn't spend the night at the hospital, but wouldn't it be better if you had an adult with you?' she asked Louisa.

'Why?' Louisa demanded, aggressively from the passenger seat. 'In case my mother dies in the middle of the night?'

No, no, of course not, tell her that wasn't what you were thinking at all, said a cautionary voice in Meadows head.

'No, not *just* for that reason – although we both accept that her dying is a possibility,' she told Louisa. 'But whatever happens, it will be so much easier to face if you've got someone else with you.'

'Someone?' Louisa said, with contempt. 'Why don't you come out with what you really mean – which is a big grown up person!'

She's looking for a fight, Meadows thought, and if it will make her feel better to lash out at someone, she can lash out at me. I'll even go against all my principles, and let her win.

'Yes, you're right, that is what I mean,' she said. 'An adult. A big grown-up person.'

'*I'm* an adult,' Louisa told her.

'If you say so,' Meadows agreed.

But Louisa seemed to have lost her taste for fighting, and simply sank back into her seat.

It was as they were pulling up at the Paniatowskis' front door that Louisa said, 'Maybe you're right, Kate – maybe it would be nice to have someone else there with me.'

'Would you like me to call one of your mother's friends for you?' Meadows asked.

Louisa laughed. 'What friends?' she asked.

Yes, it was a pretty stupid thing to say, when you thought about it, Meadows told herself.

When the boss wasn't with her team, she was with her kids – just as when she herself wasn't with the team, she was into bondage with strangers, while Beresford searched for fresh women to seduce, and Crane wrote poetry.

None of them had any real friends outside the team – because nobody outside the team could really understand them.

'Look, I'm not very good on the sympathy and understanding front – that's more in Jack Crane's line,' she said. 'To tell you the truth, your mother uses me more as an attack dog.'

'Yes, that's the impression I got,' Louisa said – and it was good to hear her giggle.

'But if you want me to stay with you overnight, Louisa, then I will,' Meadows said.

'I'd like that,' Louisa told her. 'I'd like it very much.'

Colin Beresford didn't care much for the Fox and Hounds. There was no actual tangible reason for his lack of enthusiasm – the dartboard was as well-oiled as the dartboard in any other halfway organized pub; the domino table had that comfortable and comforting worn-away look about it; the draught beer was good;

the peanuts were salty – but somehow he just didn't feel at home in it.

But then wasn't that the point? He would feel at home in the Drum and Monkey – yes! – but everybody there would be watching him and pitying him.

At least no one in the Fox and Hounds knew who he was.

At least there, he could be alone with his misery.

And he had plenty of misery to contemplate. For almost his entire career in the Mid Lancs police, Monika Paniatowski had been at his side. She had been his guide, his teacher and his friend, and, more than once, she had put her own job on the line to save his. There was a time when he'd thought he was in love with her. He didn't believe that any longer – or, at least, there was only a tiny part of him that still did – but he certainly did *love* her, more than anyone else in the world.

Beresford checked his watch. Jack Crane should be arriving soon, though Kate Meadows, who was with Louisa, had not been sure whether or not she could make it. Well, it didn't really matter whether she could or not, because until they'd been to the briefing session the following morning, they would have very little to talk about anyway.

It was time for the local early evening news, and the landlord of the Fox and Hounds reached for the long pole that he used to press the buttons on the television set, which was mounted high above the bar.

The screen came to life just as the local news was starting. As was only to be expected, the attack on DCI Paniatowski was the main news item covered. The newsreader outlined the details of the attack, and read out the telephone number that anyone with any information on the incident should call.

Then, he disappeared from the screen and was replaced by a photograph of a young blonde-haired woman, looking rather self-conscious, in a police cadet's uniform.

'DCI Paniatowski joined the Mid Lancs police as soon as she was old enough to do so,' a disembodied voice said. 'For a couple of years, she conscientiously pounded the beat like any other officer, but her real ambition was to join the CID, and, in fact, she became the first female detective sergeant in the region. For a number of years, she worked with DCI Woodend, who many viewers will surely remember as one of the more colourful characters . . .'

It was a good idea to do it this way, Beresford thought, because it got potential witnesses to see Monika as a person – it made them want to help catch her attacker, not merely because it was their duty, but because they liked her. Yes, it was a *good* idea – one that Monika would probably have approved of herself – but it sounded to him awfully like an obituary.

'You see what happens when you let women into the police force?' asked a loud voice from further up the bar.

'What does happen?' asked his friend.

'Well, they can't look after themselves, can they? They're worse than bloody useless.'

Steady, Colin, Beresford told himself – stay steady.

'I mean, for every woman you've got who's a bobby, you've got to have a male bobby whose main job it is to look after her.'

Beresford had heard of people seeing red when they were angry, and he had always thought it was no more than a figure of speech – but it was no literary device which was turning the glasses behind the bar a deep claret colour.

Calm down, Colin, he urged himself. The worst thing you can do now is go over the top.

'Not that I'm saying women bobbies aren't useful,' the idiot further along the bar continued. 'No, I wouldn't say that at all. Somebody's got to make the tea, haven't they? And if a *real* bobby – a male bobby – feels like a shag at the end of his shift, it's nice if there's someone close at hand to oblige him.'

Beresford stepped away from the bar, so he could get a look at the other man. It was no surprise to discover that he was a big feller in his thirties, the sort of man who could never – even if he'd been wearing thick horn-rimmed glasses and a long white coat – have been mistaken for a rocket scientist.

'With a bit of luck, what's happened to this Polish bint should serve as a warning to other women who think they can do a man's job,' the man said. And then he noticed that Beresford was glaring at him, and added aggressively, 'What do you think you're looking at, Sunshine?'

'Monika Paniatowski has worked bloody hard for this

community,' Beresford said, doing his best to keep his voice level and even. 'I think she's entitled to some respect.'

'Worked bloody hard for this community!' the man repeated, in a sarcastic voice.

'Leave it, Eddie,' one of his drinking companions urged him.

But Eddie didn't want to leave it.

'What's your interest in the woman?' he asked Beresford. 'Have you been slipping her a length yourself?'

'I was hoping to appeal to your sense of decency,' Beresford said, 'but since it seems that you don't have one . . .'

The punch was well-aimed and well-timed, and most men would have buckled and gone down. Indeed, for a moment, it looked as if that was just what Eddie might do.

But in addition to being a loud-mouthed bigot, he was also a seasoned street fighter, and he managed to roll with the punch, then right himself again.

Beresford took a couple of steps backwards, in order to give both himself and his opponent plenty of room for what would surely follow.

Eddie let out a roar, and flung himself at his attacker.

Beresford sidestepped, and as Eddie rushed past him, he delivered what felt like a most satisfactory uppercut to the other man's gut.

Eddie sank to his knees, and – like a matador who knows the bull is no longer a threat – Beresford turned disdainfully away from him.

He was not at all surprised to feel each of his arms grabbed in an iron grip, or to hear the pub's landlord growl to the men who now flanked him, 'Get the bastard out of here – and use the back way.'

He could announce the fact that he was a police officer, and they would leave him alone, Beresford thought, but he didn't want to do that because, if they reported him, he would be suspended.

Besides, it hadn't been a policeman who had hit Eddie, it had been Monika's mate – and as Monika's mate, he was prepared to take the punishment.

There was no pressing reason for DCI Dixon to stay at the scene of the crime (he had confidence in the lads conducting the search, and if anything of significance was found, they could easily contact him), but he stayed anyway, because the alternative – going home to Doris – was something he'd much prefer to postpone as long as possible.

He was not alone. Standing close by – as he was *always* standing close by his boss unless he'd been sent on some specific mission – was Detective Sergeant Higgins.

Higgins' nickname, back at headquarters, was Baby. This was not because he had smooth skin or innocent eyes – neither of those characteristics could have been ascribed to him – but because he was a baby rhino to his boss's large adult. He had heard the nickname and guessed its origin, but it didn't bother him. In fact, he was rather pleased that other people recognized how close he was to Dixon.

He didn't love his boss – not in any sexual way, anyway – but he most certainly revered him. Dixon had plucked him out of the ranks and seen to it that he was promoted to sergeant, and all he asked in return was unquestioning devotion – which was fine with Higgins, because though he had long ago decided that he could never be a great man himself, he saw no reason why he couldn't acquire a little of the greatness of others by brushing up against them.

Dixon looked around him – at the lush greenness of the early summer – then at his sergeant, who, if he didn't know any better, he would say had been in a trance for the previous twenty minutes.

'This certainly isn't a case I would have chosen for myself, Sergeant Higgins,' he said.

Higgins turned to him rather stiffly, like a robot which had just been reactivated.

'No, boss, I don't imagine it is,' he agreed.

'I see two possible pitfalls,' Dixon continued. 'The first is that we fail to make an arrest in this case – and if that happens, heads will roll.'

'If it does turn out that way, they don't necessarily have to be our heads,' Higgins pointed out.

'You mean they could just as easily be lopped off the shoulders of DCI Paniatowski's team?' Dixon asked.

'Exactly, boss.'

'Which brings me onto the second potential pitfall – if we can't solve the case and Paniatowski's team can, then we'll all look complete bloody idiots – and the last thing I want is to suspect that uniforms are sniggering behind my back as I walk down the corridor.'

'We'll have to see that doesn't happen, then, won't we, boss?' Higgins suggested.

'We will,' Dixon agreed. 'That's why I'm having Paniatowski's sergeant shadowing you.'

'Then she'll know everything I know,' Higgins pointed out.

'Yes, she will – and no more than that,' Dixon said. 'Whereas if she went her own way . . .'

'She could discover all kinds of things that she might decide to keep from us?'

'Exactly.'

'What about Beresford?'

'I've told him he's free to conduct his own investigation.'

'Isn't that a bit dangerous?'

'Not really – how much investigating can he do without any troops of his own to deploy?'

'You've really thought it out, haven't you, boss?' Higgins asked, admiringly.

'I certainly bloody hope so,' Dixon said, with just an edge of complacency to his voice.

Higgins consulted his watch.

'Don't you think it's about time we called off the search for today, boss?' he asked.

Dixon looked up at the sky. It was still bright enough, but, of course, it would be much darker in the woods.

'We'll maybe give it another fifteen minutes,' he said – and then he noticed the constable emerging from the woods at speed. 'Hello, it looks like we've found something.'

The constable drew level with them. He was gasping for breath, and his eyes were wide with excitement.

'Sir, sir, there's something in the woods that you really need to see,' he said.

The three men were called Tosh, Arthur and Freddie, and – as per the landlord's instructions – they had hustled Beresford into the alley behind the Fox and Hounds. Now, as Arthur and Freddie maintained a tight grip on Beresford's arms, Tosh began the task of pounding away at his gut.

'That's it!' Freddie said. 'Give him a real working over, Tosh.'

As the pain hit him, Beresford found himself hoping that these lads could judge just how much was enough, and that he'd be fit enough to report for duty in the morning.

'Police – stop that!' said an authoritive – though comparatively youthful – voice.

The pounding ceased, and Tosh stopped trying to realign Beresford's intestinal tract and turned to face the man who'd told him to stop.

'He started it,' he complained, nodding towards Beresford. 'He hit one of our pals for no reason at all.'

'Oh, really?' Crane said. 'Now isn't that interesting.'

Even though most of his thoughts were concentrated on the agony in his own gut, there was a small part of Beresford's brain which was registering genuine surprise, because he did not know this man – or rather, this was not the man he knew.

The Crane who he worked with was a bright lad who had the potential to become a good bobby. This Crane, on the other hand, had all the confidence and gravitas of a chief superintendent.

'So how *many* times did this feller hit this pal of yours?' Crane continued, sounding genuinely curious.

Tosh shrugged. 'A couple of times.'

'And how many times have you already hit him?'

Another shrug. 'Maybe three or four.'

'So it would seem to me that your business with him is over,' Crane suggested reasonably.

'This is a private matter,' Tosh said. 'It's got nothing at all to do with the police.'

'It's not my job to be anybody's nanny, and if it was one-on-one, I might well agree with you,' Crane said easily. 'However, since there are three of you, I really do think it's time to call a halt.'

'And what if we don't stop?' Tosh demanded, aggressively.

'Well, then, I'll have to arrest you,' Crane said.

'On your own?' Tosh asked. 'Do you think that you could manage all three of us?'

'Oh yes,' Crane said, with quiet confidence. 'Of course, I've only got one set of handcuffs, but I suppose I could improvise with a bit of wire or something.'

'Are you *sure* you're a bobby?' the puncher asked.

'I certainly was the last time I looked.'

'Then show us your warrant card.'

'I could do that,' Crane agreed, 'but if you make me go to the trouble of taking it out, I think I'll arrest you anyway.'

'You're bluffing,' Tosh said. 'The whole thing's been a bluff from start to finish.'

'Then call it,' Crane suggested.

Tosh looked questioningly at one of his mates, and then at the other.

'We've taught the sod a lesson he won't forget in a hurry,' he said. 'Let's go and have another drink.'

Without Arthur and Freddie to hold him upright, Beresford sank down into a squat. That helped to ease the pain – though not a great deal.

'Let me guess, sir – somebody said something less than flattering about the boss, and you hit him,' Crane said.

'The bastard had it coming,' Beresford groaned. 'Why didn't you show Tosh your warrant card?'

'Didn't have it with me,' Crane said. 'For the last couple of hours, I've been Jack Crane the poet, rather than DC Jack Crane – and when I'm being Jack Crane the poet, I leave my warrant card at home.'

'You're a really mixed-up bugger, aren't you?' Beresford asked.

'It takes one to know one,' Crane told him. 'I'm going to help you to your feet, and then I'm going to drive you back to your flat and assess the damage. I imagine that when I start to lift you, it will hurt like hell.'

He wasn't wrong.

Louisa was sitting in the easy chair next to her mother's hospital bed when Kate Meadows picked up a blanket and began tucking it in around her. At first, it seemed the logical thing to do – it was far easier for Meadows to tuck the blanket in than it would have been for Louisa herself to do it – but somehow, about halfway through the process, they both began to feel self-conscious.

'It's almost like becoming a child again,' Louisa said, 'and the worrying thing is that I quite like it.'

'Why wouldn't you?' Meadows asked. 'When things get really awful, a lot of people find comfort in retreating back to childhood.'

'Have you ever done that?' Louisa asked.

No, Meadows thought, but when you know you're going to be married off the day you turn sixteen, you don't have much of a childhood in the first place.

'Yes,' she said aloud, 'I've done it.'

Louisa narrowed her eyes. 'You don't *sound* as if you have,' she said.

Damn, Meadows thought, that was the problem with letting your guard down – you gave far too much away.

'All right, maybe some people have such bloody awful child-hoods that there's no refuge to be found there,' she conceded.

'In other words, you lied to me!' Louisa said accusingly.

'Yes,' Meadows confessed. 'I did – and I'm sorry.'

'Promise me that however horrible the truth is, you'll never lie to me again,' Louisa said, looking across at her mother's bed.

'I promise,' Meadows agreed.

There was an uncomfortable pause, then Louisa said, 'I know nobody can know for certain, but do *you* think Mum's going to get better?'

'I think there are some questions it's better never to ask,' Meadows replied – which was sort of in line with the promise she'd just made.

'You think I was a bloody fool back there, don't you?' Beresford asked, once they were in Crane's car.

'We both *know* you were a bloody fool back there,' Crane said. 'Expressing your own anger and frustration is a luxury you can't afford to indulge in when you should be devoting all your energy to catching the man who attacked the boss.'

'You're right,' Beresford agreed.

'So what do we know for certain?' Crane asked.

'We know that Monika was in Backend Woods on her own—' Beresford began.

'No, we don't,' Crane contradicted him. 'For all we know, she could have been on a date.'

Beresford felt a little stab of pain which was only partly attribu-table to having been beaten up.

'If she'd been seeing somebody, she'd have told me,' he said.

But would she, he wondered – would she really? Or, suspecting that he might still have some romantic affection for her, might she have decided to keep quiet about it?

'Alternatively, it could be something to do with the job,' Crane said, 'but I can't think of anything we're even vaguely interested in at the moment which would have taken her anywhere near Backend Woods. Can you?'

'No,' Beresford said.

He could, he supposed, tell Crane that he was almost certain Meadows knew why Monika had been there, but was equally sure that, since the sergeant clearly didn't believe it had anything to do with the attack, there was no way on God's green earth that she was ever going to tell them about it.

Yes, he could certainly do that – but he was just too damned tired.

He glanced down at his watch.

'Turn on Radio Whitebridge,' he said. 'There may be something new on there.'

What there was blasting out of the radio was the latest ABBA song about the pain of breaking up, but then, as it was almost approaching its climax, the DJ faded it out.

'This just in,' he said. 'Police investigating the attack on DCI Monika Paniatowski have found the body of a young woman in Backend Woods. More details as soon as we have them.'

ABBA filled the airspace again, and for at least ten seconds, both Beresford and Crane sat in shocked silence.

Then Beresford said, 'Jesus, this changes everything!'

FOUR

Monday

During the night, there had been some clouds in the sky, but apart from a few of the wispier ones – which had floated across the moon like veils shed by an erotic dancer – they had been scarcely noticeable, and come the morning, there was no evidence of them at all. In fact, it was one of those rare days in Lancashire (famous for its rain) when the sky was a perfect blue. It was the sort of day when people said, 'lovely day for a walk,' or 'lovely day for getting that bit of gardening done,' but down at Whitebridge police headquarters, nobody – not a single officer – said, 'lovely day for a murder investigation.'

The press briefing room was located on the ground floor, very close to the headquarters' main entrance. This was at least partly based on the theory that while journalist and television reporters were, of course, all fine chaps (and chapesses), who were, moreover, dedicated only to finding the truth, and consequently more than eager to work with the police in a spirit of true co-operation – blah, blah, blah – it was probably best to keep the slimy untrustworthy bastards (and bitches) as far away from the nerve centre of the building as possible.

The two men giving the press conference – at the ungodly hour of eight o'clock in the morning – were Chief Constable Pickering and DCI Dixon. Pickering wore the smart uniform he normally reserved for ceremonial occasions. Dixon was wearing a smart blue suit which either came from Savile Row or was an outstanding imitation.

Facing them were all the local hacks, plus a smattering of national newspaper reporters (an attack on a senior police officer, even in a backwater like Whitebridge, was still big news) and three television crews.

As was his privilege, Pickering opened the proceedings, then quickly handed over to Dixon.

'Following the attack on DCI Paniatowski, officers searching the woodland area discovered the body of a girl aged between sixteen and eighteen,' Dixon said. 'She had been strangled.' He paused, to let this information sink in, before continuing, 'A sketch of her has since been released.' Dixon paused again, while the artist's impression (free from any of the ugly contortions of death which a photograph would have revealed) filled the projector screen. 'Forensics would seem to indicate that she died sometime within the two hours before DCI Paniatowski's attack,' the detective chief inspector continued. 'We have appealed for anyone who might know her to come forward, but she has yet to be identified.' He glanced at his watch. 'As you can imagine, we have a busy day ahead of us, ladies and gentlemen, but I'm willing to take a few questions now.'

'Do you think DCI Paniatowski was attacked because she saw the murder?' a reporter from a London tabloid asked.

'Anything is possible,' Dixon said, 'but it's highly unlikely. DCI Paniatowski was – is – a highly trained and very experienced officer. I cannot believe that having seen the killer in the act, she would then allow him to sneak up behind her, and smash her head in with a stone.'

Colin Beresford, who was watching the press conference on a monitor with Sergeant Higgins, heard the words, and shuddered.

DCI Paniatowski was – is – a highly trained and very experienced officer.

He'd talked to the hospital himself, and while they wouldn't give him any details – since he wasn't a relative – they'd at least given him to understand that he needn't necessarily be thinking about getting out his black tie yet.

Yet everyone else seemed to take it as read that Monika wouldn't recover.

Why was that?

Because they were much more realistic than he was?

Or because it was a northern trait to always expect the worst?

'Had the killer hidden the body?' one of the reporters asked.

'There had been some attempt to hide the girl, but it was half-hearted at best,' Dixon told him. 'We think that the killer had either not planned to take his victim's life or had suddenly realized that – for some reason – he did not have enough time to make a proper job of concealing her.'

'Had the dead girl been sexually assaulted in any way?' asked the man from the BBC.

Dixon shook his head. 'There is nothing at all to suggest she had been molested in that way,' he said.

'Does your boss normally do this?' Beresford asked DS Higgins.

'Do what?'

'Show his whole hand right at the beginning.'

'Come again?'

'He's made it public knowledge, right from the start, that the girl's been strangled, and that she wasn't sexually assaulted.'

'So?'

'So whatever happened to holding information back, so we'll have a way of testing whether anybody who calls in about the murder has something useful to say, or just a nutter?'

'Let me see if I've got this straight, *sir*,' DS Higgins said, with a dangerous edge creeping into his voice. 'You're saying that my boss doesn't know what he's doing, are you?'

He'd forgotten he was no more than a barely-tolerated visitor on this team, and so he had gone too far, Beresford realized.

'No, I wouldn't suggest that at all,' he said. 'Or if I did, I was quite wrong. Mr Dixon is an experienced high-ranking officer, so it was foolish of me to assume he'd shown his whole hand.' He paused for a second. 'He *is* holding something back, isn't he?'

Higgins smiled. 'Of course he is.'

Beresford waited for the sergeant to say more, but it soon became plain that he wasn't about to do that.

His best course of action was do likewise – to steer clear of any situation in which there was potential for him to lose face – he told himself, but there was an undisciplined goblin within him which forced him to say, 'So what is it that he's holding back?'

'All will be revealed at the briefing,' Higgins said.

'Why can't you tell me now,' Beresford heard the goblin say.

'Why can't I tell you now, sir?' Higgins repeated. 'I can't tell you now because we're both on DCI Dixon's team, which means we play by DCI Dixon's rules – and one of those rules is that his unworthy underlings – like me – don't say anything until he's told us we *can* say it.'

She is in the woods – or maybe even a forest.

The ground feels spongy under her feet, and her nostrils are filled with the smell of damp ferns.

She knows it's important that she's there, but she doesn't know why it's important.

It bothers her that the trees don't look like they should – are different to the ones in . . . the ones in . . . the ones in wherever she is now.

No, she doesn't mean that, either.

Where she is now is in the woods.

What she wants to say is, different to ones near where she lives.

She wishes she knew why she was here – in this place with trees which are as foreign to her as . . . as she doesn't know what.

And suddenly there is a sound – a dull thudding, regular sound, vibrating across the woodland floor.

Then she sees them – the man and the horse.

The horse is a chestnut mare.

How does she know it's a mare at this distance?

She really couldn't say.

The man is wearing the scarlet and blue uniform of a Polish cavalry officer. He has seen her, and canters up to where she is standing.

Looking up at the horse – seeing which part of it is at her eye level – she realizes she must have shrunk since the morning.

The man reaches down and swings her into the saddle, as if she weighed nothing.

She can smell the leather of his boots. She can feel the slight tickle as his chin bristles brush against her soft skin.

She knows who he is now – he's her father.

But he's dead – mowed down as he foolishly, but heroically, led his company in a charge against German machine guns.

Yes, he's dead, so he can't be the reason she's here.

It is all so confusing.

Meadows watched Louisa carefully guiding her two half-brothers down the stairs – each with one of his tiny hands in her much larger ones.

The girl had a natural air of authority about her, and it had clearly never occurred to either of them to seriously challenge that authority yet – but when one of them did, Meadows suspected, it would be Thomas, who seemed much more aware than his brother of the power that was growing in him.

It was impossible to say whether or not they had the same father, she thought, though that, too, might become clearer as they grew older.

Meadows had once briefly met all three of the possible fathers (and, for a while, had carried their testicles around in a plastic bag), but she could not see any of those men reflected back to her in the faces of the twins.

'I'm going to switch on the television, to hear what they're saying about the attack,' Louisa told Meadows.

Meadows frowned. 'Are you sure that's wise?' she asked.

'Why wouldn't it be?' Louisa wondered.

Because it'll get you thinking about your mother, lying helpless in that hospital room, Meadows thought – and that's the last thing I want.

'It might upset the twins,' she said.

'Bullshit!' Louisa retorted. She looked rather shocked that the word had escaped from her own mouth, but having set it free, she said briskly, 'the twins are too young to understand what's going on. But you weren't really thinking about them at all, were you?'

'No,' Meadows said, and wondered why, when she could put the fear into almost anyone she came into contact with, this kid found it so easy to ride roughshod over her.

'I have to get used to the possibility that Mum might die,' Louisa said. 'I have to be ready for it.'

'She's not going to die,' Meadows said.

'You don't know that,' Louisa replied, with a calm that was almost icy. 'I have to be ready for it – I must be prepared.'

She led the boys to the table, hoisted them into their chairs, and began preparing their cereal.

Meadows glanced down at her watch. 'Look, I've got to go,' she said.

'That's all right,' Louisa said. 'Elena and I can manage.'

'Well, I'll . . . I'll call in again later,' Meadows said uncomfortably.

'That would be nice,' Louisa told her.

Once the sergeant had gone, Louisa's poise collapsed. It started with a slight wobble of her chin, then the pricking tears in her eyes, until finally a wave of despair washed over her entire body.

'Louisa?' Thomas said worriedly.

'I'm all right, Tommy,' Louisa said, wiping away the tears with one hand and rubbing the top of his head with the other. 'Honestly.'

She was not feeling as brave as she'd been when Meadows was there, but she knew that what she'd said then had been true, and was no less true now.

She had to prepare herself for the worst!

She crossed the room on legs that had suddenly turned to wood, and raised an arm impeded by invisible weights until it was high enough to switch the television on.

Rhino Dixon's head appeared on the screen. In fact, it *filled* the screen, in a way you just knew no other head would quite be able to do.

'Following the attack on DCI Paniatowski, officers searching the woodland area discovered the body of a girl aged between sixteen and eighteen. A picture of her has since been released,' Dixon said.

An artist's impression replaced the chief superintendent's head, though his voice continued to provide the background music.

'Forensics would seem to indicate that she died . . .'

'Well, bugger me sideways!' Louisa said.

The team briefing had been scheduled for immediately after the press briefing, and so, half a minute after the monitor went dead, the door to the CID suite swung open and Dixon marched in.

'What did you think of my performance, Sergeant Higgins?' he demanded.

'It was very good, sir,' the sergeant replied.

'Yes, it was, wasn't it,' Dixon agreed. He ran his eyes over his own team, and then settled on Crane and Beresford.

'Where's your sergeant, Inspector Beresford?' he asked. 'Is this maybe a bit too early in the morning for her? Does she need a couple of hours to put on her face before she comes to work?'

'Meadows doesn't wear much make-up, sir,' he said, knowing it was the wrong answer – but angry enough, on Meadows's behalf, not to give a damn. 'In fact, I don't think she wears any.'

At least, not in the daytime, he added mentally, but at night – when she's Zelda, the bringer of pain and pleasure – it's a very different story.

'Are you trying to be funny, inspector?' Dixon asked.

'No, sir, just answering your question,' Beresford said. 'But perhaps a better answer would have been that she spent the night at the hospital, with Louisa.'

'Louisa?'

'DCI Paniatowski's daughter. Meadows felt there should be someone with her.'

'There probably should have been,' Dixon agreed, 'but Meadows does know that we're the police force, not the social services department, doesn't she?'

'Yes, sir, that's the other reason she was there – she thought Louisa might know something which could help the investigation, and not even be aware of it.'

Dixon clapped his hands – briefly, but appreciatively.

'That's the best excuse I've heard in a long time. It's a real thoroughbred, is that.' He turned to Higgins. 'Would you like to brief us, sergeant?'

'The body was found just before dark, last night,' Higgins said. 'It was decided to acknowledge the discovery, but to release very few details until this morning.'

'I half-expected not to have to release an artist's impression at all,' Dixon said. 'I thought that once we'd announced we'd found the body, anybody whose kid hadn't come home at the right time would ring us. But it didn't happen, did it, sergeant?'

'A few of the usual cranks phoned up – but that was about it.'

'Five minutes from now, it will be a different story,' Dixon promised. 'The switchboards are probably already jammed. Anyway, carry on, sergeant.'

'At the moment, we've got a lot more questions than answers,' Higgins admitted. 'We're hopeful we'll find out who she is in the next hour or so, but that still doesn't tell us why she was up at the hall, or how she got there. What we also don't know is *why* he did *what* he did after her death.'

'I said at the press conference that she hadn't been sexually assaulted, because I don't think what happened *was* a sexual assault, though it's possible the experts will disagree with me later,' Dixon said. He lit a cigarette, and inhaled deeply, as if he really needed something to distract him. 'After the victim was dead – and Dr Shastri is convinced this *was* post mortem – the killer rolled down her panties and – and these are Dr Shastri's words – sluiced out her vagina with a liquid so hot that it caused extensive blistering. Then he rolled her panties back up again. Now did he do it as a punishment? Hardly – unless he didn't know she was dead. And why put the panties back on? That shows a degree of respect totally at odds with drenching her fanny in boiling tea.'

'Tea?' somebody gasped. 'Did you say tea, boss?'

'That's right,' Dixon agreed. 'We can't be sure until it's been tested, but the doc's almost certain the liquid used was tea.'

'We also don't know why the killer attacked DCI Paniatowski,' Higgins added, 'because, as the boss said at the press conference, she can't have seen the murder, or she'd never have left herself so open to attack like that.'

'And why did he use a stone to attack the chief inspector?' Dixon said. 'Why didn't he just strangle her? Wasn't he confident of his own strength?'

'Maybe he'd have thought it was sacrilegious, sir,' Crane whispered to Beresford.

'What's that you're saying?' asked Dixon, who, even when he was facing in the opposite direction, seemed to miss nothing.

'It was just a thought, sir – probably not worth mentioning,' Crane said awkwardly.

'On the contrary, if you've got a theory, we'd love to hear it,' Dixon said. 'We're always willing to listen to *anything* that an Oxford University graduate wants to tell us.'

Now how the bloody hell did the chief super know about that? Crane wondered. The only people who were *supposed* to know were Paniatowski, Beresford and Meadows.

'Well?' Dixon demanded.

'It's possible the girl's killing was a ritual one, sir,' he said.

'What makes you think that?'

'What he did to her after she was dead.'

'Fair point,' Dixon agreed. 'And how does that relate to the attack on DCI Paniatowski?'

'In a ritual killing, the killer rarely dislikes the victim,' Crane said. 'On the contrary, he often holds the victim in high esteem, and the manner in which he kills is a way of showing his respect.'

'And because DCI Paniatowski wasn't part of the ritual, she couldn't be strangled?' Dixon asked.

'That's right,' Crane agreed. 'He wouldn't have considered her worthy of that particular death.'

'And she'd miss out on the hot tea as well?'

'Undoubtedly, sir. That would be like giving the last rites to a dog – it would degrade the whole process.'

The door opened, and a WPC entered the room, carrying a sheet of paper which she handed directly to Dixon.

The chief inspector read it once, read it a second time, then looked up at Beresford.

'You did say that DCI Paniatowski has a daughter, called Louisa, didn't you, inspector?' he asked.

'Yes, sir.'

'And would you say she's a sensible kind of girl?'

'Very sensible. She's thinking of becoming a police cadet, and I don't think she'd have any difficulty with the selection board.'

'Interesting,' Dixon mused, 'because, you see, she's just phoned up to say that the dead girl is called Mary Green, and that Mary and her brother John are both in Louisa's class at school.'

The same WPC returned with another piece of paper. 'And it seems that young Louisa is right,' Dixon said, 'because we've now had another six calls – all of which identify the girl as Mary Green.' He frowned. 'The really interesting question is, why wasn't one of those calls from her mum and dad?'

FIVE

I f Balaclava Street had been named after the battle in the Crimean War – which seemed more than likely, Meadows thought – then the rows of mill workers' terraced cottages which lined it were around 120 years old.

The houses themselves were still structurally sound, but this street – and perhaps a couple of dozen other streets just like it – were still doomed, because though the two-up-two-downs were once regarded as 'little palaces' by those who lived in them, they fell well short of modern expectations.

Meadows parked her Mini Cooper in front of number 29, which was where, according to her school records, Mary Green lived.

She quickly examined the front door (painted a standard navy blue), and the pattern on the curtains hanging in the front windows (daffodils and snowdrops) – and decided there was nothing unusual there.

She turned to the man in the passenger seat and said, 'Since – as you've been at pains to point out – this is more your investigation than it is ours, I expect you'll be handling this interview, will you, DS Higgins?'

Higgins shrugged. 'In this sort of situation, I always feel the feminine touch is more appropriate,' he said awkwardly.

'Meaning that you haven't got the stomach to tell a mother that her daughter is probably dead?' Meadows asked.

Higgins forced a grin to his face. 'That's men for you,' he said. The grin vanished so quickly it might never have been there. 'Seriously,' he continued, 'the worse it's handled, the less we're likely to get out of it – which is why, on this occasion, I think you should be in charge.'

'In that case, let's do it,' Meadows said, and since she was not encumbered by a seat belt (as the more safety conscious DS Higgins was) she was already knocking on the door of number 29 by the time the other sergeant had got fully out of the car.

The woman who answered Meadow's knock was around forty years old. She was not particularly attractive, but she was not particularly ugly, either. She was wearing a floral pinafore (as, in all probability, were most of the housewives on Balaclava Street at that time of day), and she looked quite unnerved to find a stranger standing at her front door.

'Mrs Green?' Meadows asked, as she held out her warrant card.

'Yes?' the woman replied, somehow managing to make her answer seem more like a question.

'We're here to ask you a few questions about your daughter,' Meadows explained. 'Do you think we could come inside?'

'Mary's at school, so I don't really see the point . . .' Mrs Green began, but as Meadows continued walking towards her, apparently completely unaware that as things stood, a collision was inevitable, she decided she had no choice but to retreat down her hallway – and as soon as she'd done that, Meadows and Higgins were inside the house, too.

'You'd better go into the parlour, while I fetch my husband,' Mrs Green said, indicating the door to the left, before carrying on herself to the back of the house, where the kitchen was.

Meadows and Higgins exchanged glances, then mutually decided to do as they'd been instructed.

'Well, this is like being in a time machine,' said Higgins, who was local and essentially working class.

'What do you mean?' asked Meadows – who was not even close to being either of those things.

'It used to be, round here, that the parlour was the best room, used only for christenings, weddings and funerals,' Higgins explained. 'It didn't matter how big the family was, you made do with the other three rooms, and kept your parlour pristine. Well, of course, that's all gone now – people have more sense and care more about their comfort than appearances – but it hasn't gone *here*, has it?'

Meadows looked around. The print hanging over the mantelpiece was called *The Chinese Girl*, and had once been so popular that half the front parlours in the country seemed to have one. Below the mantelpiece, a fan had been made out of wallpaper, and placed in the empty fireplace. On the wall opposite the print, three painted plaster ducks of different sizes were frozen, mid-flight, on their journey to the ceiling. The three-piece was not new, but looked unused; the rug in front of the hearth was made of heavy crocheted wool.

'It's like a museum, isn't it?' Higgins asked.

'Or an Alfred Hitchcock film set,' Meadows said – and though she did not make a habit of shuddering, she shuddered then.

She had been getting the feeling that there was something missing, and now she realized what it was.

'Have the people who keep their front parlours like this got something against photographs?' she asked.

'No, of course they haven't,' Higgins said, his tone suggesting that if she didn't already know that, then she had no chance of ever understanding the north. 'We put great store by photos round here. Why, even when there was real poverty, families still managed to scrape enough to go to a professional photographer, and . . .' He stopped, mid-flow, and looked around him. 'There aren't any photos in here, are there?'

'No,' Meadows agreed, 'there are not.'

There was the sound of footsteps in the hallway, then a middle-aged man in a blue boiler suit appeared in the doorway.

'I'm Mr Green,' he said. 'You're lucky to have caught me, because normally, at this time of day, I'd already be at work.'

Meadows ran her eyes up and down the boiler suit for signs of the company logo, but it didn't appear to be bearing one.

'Now what's all this about our Mary?' Mr Green asked.

'I take it that you haven't watched any television this morning,' Meadows said.

'We don't own a television, do we, Mother?' Mr Green said.

'No, we don't,' came his wife's voice from the corridor.

'And you haven't looked at the newspaper?'

'We don't take a newspaper, either,' said Mrs Green's disembodied voice.

'When was the last time you saw your daughter?' Meadows asked.

'Why do you want to know?' Mr Green countered.

'Please just answer the question,' Meadows said, with a new – more commanding – edge to her voice.

'It must have been yesterday morning,' Mr Green said.

'So she was out for most of the day?'

'Yes.'

'Weren't you worried when she didn't come home last night?'

'How do you know she didn't come home?'

'Please, Mr Green, just do it my way, and all will soon become clear,' Meadows said.

'No, I wasn't worried when she didn't come home last night, because I wasn't expecting her to come home. At weekends, she looks after Mrs Brown, who is practically bedridden, and on Monday mornings, she goes straight from there to school. So I don't see why you're—'

'I'm afraid I may have some bad news for you,' Meadows said.

Up to that point, Green had merely sounded defensive, but now an element of alarm crept into his voice.

'What . . . what kind of bad news?' he asked.

'It's possible your daughter may have been murdered.'

Green shook his head. 'No, you're wrong, that isn't possible. It couldn't have happened to one of us.'

'One of us?' Meadows repeated. 'What do you mean by that?'

But before Green had had time to answer, Higgins had unrolled the artist's impression, and was holding it out for him to inspect.

'Is this your daughter, Mary?' he asked.

'No,' Green replied, giving the sketch no more than a cursory glance. 'No, it's not her.'

Mrs Green appeared in the doorway, and, elbowing her husband out of the way, glanced down at the sketch.

'Oh my God!' she groaned. 'Oh sweet Jesus!'

'Now, Joan, this is just an artist's impression, and we all know how misleading they can be,' her husband said.

But Joan Green seemed to have absolutely no doubt at all.

'This is Satan's work,' she said – to no one in particular. 'He has tracked us down, and now the slaughter begins.'

'Joan . . .' said Mr Green, ineffectually.

'Mother!' said a louder, firmer voice, and a new figure appeared in the corridor – a tall young man, dressed in a yellow jumper and jeans, who looked vaguely familiar.

The young man put his hands on his mother's shoulder, and half-eased, half-dragged her into the corridor. Once he had her there, he turned his attention to his father, and said, 'Take her into the kitchen and make her a good strong cup of tea, Dad.'

'Now just a minute—' DS Higgins began.

'I'll tell you anything you need to know,' the young man interrupted him, as he ushered his father into the corridor. 'Won't you at least give my mum and dad a few minutes on their own, to get over the shock?'

'I suppose we could,' Higgins said, dubiously. 'But that would mean putting a lot of responsibility on you.'

'I can handle it,' the young man said.

At the sound of the kitchen door being closed behind his parents, a look of relief crossed his face. He held out his hand to Higgins and said, 'I'm John Green, and, as you've probably gathered by now, I'm Mary's brother.'

'You do know, don't you, John, that in all likelihood, your sister Mary is dead?'

John Green nodded, sombrely.

'I've seen the picture. I know it's her.'

'You seem remarkably calm,' Meadows said.

'I have to be calm,' John Green said, 'just as, if I'd been the one who'd been murdered, Mary would have had to be calm. We've known, from the moment we stopped being little babies, that it was always going to be a case of us looking after our parents, rather than the other way round.' He paused. 'But that doesn't mean I'm not gutted. I loved my sister – I always will.'

'How did your sister end up in Backend Woods?' Meadows asked.

'I honestly have no idea,' John Green confessed. 'She should have been looking after Mrs Brown all day yesterday. Mrs Brown is practically bedridden, you know.'

'Do you take turns?' Meadows wondered.

'I don't know what you mean.'

'Do you and your sister take it in turns to look after Mrs Brown at the weekends?'

'No, of course not,' John Green said.

'So she got to keep all the money herself.'

'What money?'

'The money Mrs Brown paid her.'

'Mrs Brown didn't pay her anything. Mary did it out of the goodness of her heart.'

'Is that because she saw it as her Christian duty?'

'She isn't – she wasn't – a Christian. None of us are.'

'And yet your mother said, "Oh God, no," and thought that your sister had been killed by Satan himself.'

'That's just a figure of speech,' John Green said. 'My parents aren't exactly militant atheists – they haven't got the spirit or the fire to be militant *anythings* – but we've never been to church, we don't get Easter eggs, and even Christmas is hardly celebrated in this house.'

'Anyway, you're saying that you don't help out with Mrs Brown,' Meadows said.

'That's right.'

'Because there is no goodness in your heart?'

'Because it's a job that girls are better at than boys.'

'So where were you, yesterday?' Higgins asked.

'Do you think I killed my own sister?' John Green asked, outraged.

'Not necessarily,' DS Higgins told him. 'If you want the truth, I consider the prospect that you killed her to be highly unlikely. But I'd still like to know where you were yesterday.'

'I was at seventeen Inkerman Street from ten in the morning until nine thirty in the evening.'

'That's quite a long time to be anywhere that isn't your home,' DS Higgins said.

'Is it?'

'What were you doing there?'

'I was visiting a friend.'

'I'll need his name.'

'Roger Smith.'

'Do you go to school with him?'

'No.'

'So which school does he go to?'

'He doesn't go to school at all.'

'Why not?'

'Possibly because of his age.'

'How old is he?'

'I couldn't say for sure,' John Green said, 'but I would guess that he must be around fifty.'

Higgins raised a questioning eyebrow in Meadows's general direction.

'Was Mrs Smith there?' he asked.

'Roger isn't married.'

'So it was just the two of you, then?'

'No, Michael Gray and Philip Jones were also there.'

'And are they as old as Mr Smith?'

'No, they're my age.'

'I see,' Higgins said, scratching his head thoughtfully. 'And what were the four of you doing all that time?'

'We were playing Diplomacy.'

'What's that?'

'It's a board game.'

'And you were playing it for nearly twelve hours?'

'Yes.'

'How many games did you play?'

'Just the one.'

'If you're going to lie, at least be clever about it,' Higgins said. 'No game lasts that long.'

Meadows was wondering whether it was better to contradict Higgins or to allow him to carry on making a fool of himself. She'd lose out either way, she decided.

'Games of Diplomacy can often last that long,' she said.

DS Higgins looked at her through suspicious eyes. 'You did say it was a board game, didn't you?' he said, as if he wanted to make absolutely sure he had his facts right before he went on the attack again.

'That's right,' Meadows agreed.

'I've played Monopoly, and there's no way that a game of Monopoly could last for nearly twelve hours,' Higgins said.

'Diplomacy isn't like Monopoly,' Meadows replied. 'There are no dice and you don't draw any cards. In fact, there's no element of chance in it at all.'

'How does it work, then?' Higgins demanded.

'Since you've played it more recently than I have, maybe you should explain,' Meadows said to John Green.

'The board is a map of Europe,' John said. 'The game starts in 1901, although, strictly speaking, the map corresponds more to the situation in 1914, and—'

'What the hell's he talking about?' Higgins asked Meadows.

'Each player is one of the Great Powers,' Meadows said, deciding to draw John Green away from the firing line. 'You start out with a given number of armies and navies, but if you wish to increase the size of your armed forces, you must instruct one of your armies to occupy one of the neutral territories for a whole campaign season.'

'And it's as simple as that, is it?' Higgins asked, clearly still disbelieving her.

'No, of course it isn't,' Meadows said. 'Since in the initial stages of the game you're not strong enough to bully the other powers, you have to persuade one or two of them to support your occupation.'

'And why would they do that?'

'Because you offer them something in return.'

'So how do you ever get the upper hand?'

'You wait for the right moment, then you stab your allies in the back.' Her own attempt at 'diplomacy' clearly wasn't pacifying her unasked-for and unwanted partner, Meadows thought – so why not have a bit of fun instead? 'Doesn't that all sound rather familiar to you?' she continued.

'How do you mean?' Higgins asked.

Meadows smiled sweetly. 'Well, isn't it more or less the same game that ambitious sergeants play virtually all the time, down at police headquarters?'

For a moment, it looked as if DS Higgins might say something he would later regret. Then he changed his mind and turned his attention back to John Green.

'I'm going to need the names and addresses of all these "friends" of yours,' he said.

'Of course,' John Green agreed.

'And your parents are going to have to identify the body. Do you want to tell them that yourself, or should I ask DS Meadows to do it?'

Green had been very much in control of himself – and perhaps of the interview – up to this point, but now his eyes were filling with tears and his chin had started to wobble.

'Couldn't I do it instead?' he asked. 'Couldn't *I* identify the body?'

'How old are you?' Higgins said.

'Seventeen.'

'Then you're not an adult in the eyes of the law, and we need an adult to make a formal identification.'

'But I don't know if they'll be able to cope,' John said, and now he really was crying. 'You see, we never . . . we never thought this would happen.'

Louisa sat in the living room, cradling Philip in her arms, and keeping a watchful eye on Thomas, as he roamed with wild abandon across the floor, in search of objects with which to harm himself.

She had not slept well, and now her arm was tired, her head was pounding, and every time she thought about her mother she felt her chest heave and her heart beat out a drum solo.

She needed a break, and now that her mother was in hospital, she was unofficially the head of the household, so she could, if she wished, instruct Elena to take over.

Instruct?

No, that would never do. She could *ask* Elena to take over.

Yet she didn't feel comfortable doing it – was simply not happy to assume the role of boss over a girl who was actually a couple of years older than her, because it just didn't feel right.

Yes, Elena was having a better life in Whitebridge than she would probably have had in the Spanish village, near Benidorm, from which Louisa's biological mother's family hailed. And, yes, she'd been given time off to take all kinds of educational courses, which would help her be more successful once she was back in Spain. But all the same, to treat someone like a servant, even if that was actually what they were . . .

'Give Felipe to me,' said a voice, and when Louisa looked up, she saw Elena standing there.

'I'm fine with him,' she said.

'You are not fine,' Elena said bluntly. 'If you do not believe me, take a look at your face in the mirror.'

'But if I've not got Philip and Thomas to look after, what will I do?' Louisa fretted.

'Go to school,' Elena said.

'I couldn't do that!'

'You must. There you will have an . . . an *estructura*.'

'A structure?'

'Yes. You will know what to do there. Here, it take all your effort not to cry, and pretty soon, the babies are gonna notice.'

Louisa felt a huge wave of relief surge through her whole body.

'If you're sure . . .' she began.

'*Madre de Dios*, do you want me to have it tattooed on my arm?' Elena asked, exasperatedly.

'I'll go upstairs and get changed,' Louisa said.

'Good idea,' Elena agreed.

The Incident Room (a.k.a. the basement) in Whitebridge police headquarters had undergone one of those rapid transformations it always underwent when a major crime had been committed. Barriers, road signs and other routine policing paraphernalia had been cleared out (God alone knew where to!), desks, chairs, a blackboard and a podium had been moved in, and by the time detective inspectors Beresford and Marsden arrived, all the chairs were occupied, some by local officers, others by men who had been drafted in from other divisions.

Having made a similar entrance perhaps a couple of dozen times, Beresford was almost at the podium before he realized it wasn't *his* podium, because this wasn't *his* incident room.

'Would you like to take a seat, inspector?' Marsden invited.

Oh no, that would never do, Beresford thought.

To sit there amongst the detective constables, while another DI stood on the podium and briefed his troops – with the godlike certainty that whatever he wanted done would *be* done – really wasn't on at all.

'I think I'll stand by the door,' he said.

Marsden shrugged. 'Please yourself.'

Beresford turned on his heel, and retreated the three or four steps to the door. And there, for the duration of the briefing, he intended to stay – a part of the investigation, if not quite part of the team.

He watched Marsden mount the podium. They were about the same age, he guessed (though Marsden's thick black beard made him seem older), and they were roughly the same height. Marsden, he believed, was married with kids, but he didn't know the other man well enough to say for certain that he was right about that.

Marsden looked down at all the expectant faces below him. 'For those of you who don't know me, I'm DI Marsden,' he said. 'You're here because a young girl has been murdered, and one of our own has been put into hospital with injuries from which she may never recover. Now it shouldn't be necessary to say that I expect your best work from you, so I won't – but God help you if that isn't exactly what I get from you.'

That's the wrong way to introduce yourself to the team, Beresford thought – totally the wrong way.

Oh really, asked an unexpected – and certainly unwelcome – voice from the back of his head? Is it really wrong? Or is it that you just wouldn't do it that way yourself, Colin?

It may just be that I wouldn't do it that way myself, Beresford admitted, with some chagrin.

'We now have the rough figures for visitors to Stamford Hall on Sunday – and they're not exactly encouraging,' Marsden was telling the detective constables. He turned to DS Yates – a respected veteran and safe pair of hands – who would be handling the nuts and bolts of running the incident room, and said, 'Tell us the worst, Graham.'

I wouldn't have handled it like that at all, Beresford thought. I'd never have said the figures weren't encouraging – I'd have called them a challenge.

Well that's just you, isn't it? the voice asked. Lesser mortals just have to do the best they can.

'Eight hundred and five cars and twenty-seven motorbikes entered the grounds through the West Gate,' DS Yates said. 'That's over three thousand three hundred visitors already. There were also fifteen chartered coaches, which, at sixty passengers a coach, is another nine hundred. And in addition, there were shuttle buses from the railway station, which brought in another four hundred. That's a lot of potential suspects.'

'Whoever was initially in charge of the crime scene was sensible enough to follow standard procedures and take the names and addresses of all the drivers who left after DCI Paniatowski's body – I mean, after DCI *Paniatowski* – was found, but there were at least a hundred who had already left before that,' DI Marsden said. 'We've put out an appeal, asking them to contact us, and also appealed for anybody who arrived by shuttle bus to come forward. We expect, based on previous experience, that something like a half of them will. The rest, of course, won't want their neat little lives inconvenienced just because there's been a murder. As far as the coaches go, most of them were hired by social clubs and similar organizations, so we expect to have a list of those visitors fairly soon.'

'We have had one bit of luck,' DS Yates said. 'As you all know, closed circuit television cameras are still a bit of a rarity in Lancashire, but the earl got some installed a couple of years ago, when he was holding that big pop concert of his. So what that means is that every vehicle that entered or left that day is on tape, and – barring accidents – we should have all the licence plates, once somebody's gone through the tapes.'

'That sounds like just the job for DC Crane, with his university education,' DI Marsden said. He turned to look at Beresford. 'Do you have any objection to us using DC Crane, DI Beresford?'

'None at all,' Beresford replied, though the voice inside his head was saying, 'Sod you, you bloody bastard!'

'I want everyone who was there on Sunday questioned comprehensively, and I want all the interviews cross-referenced,' Marsden said. 'The killer will be on one of those lists, and I don't want him slipping through our fingers. Sergeant Yates will give you your specific assignments. That's all for now.'

He stepped down from the podium, and headed for the door. He looked surprised to see Beresford was still there, and even more surprised when it became clear that the other inspector wasn't going to move out of the way in order to let him leave.

'Do you have a problem, DI Beresford?' he asked.

'No,' Beresford replied, '*we* have a problem – and it's not one I want to talk through where we can be overheard.'

Beresford and Marsden strode to the far end of the car park, where they were screened from the main headquarters building by several large police vans.

'Is this private enough for you?' Marsden asked.

Beresford looked around. Not only was there no one in earshot, there wasn't even anyone in sight.

'It'll do fine,' he said.

'So what's on your mind?'

'Don't you ever do that to me again,' Beresford said.

'Don't ever do what to you again?' Marsden replied, wonderingly – though Beresford was sure he knew exactly what he was talking about.

'Don't ever put me in a position where I'm forced to agree with you, whether or not I think you're right.'

'Is this about me giving the job of checking the tapes to DC Crane?' Marsden asked.

'You know it is.'

'What's the matter? Don't you think he's up to it? If that's the problem, I can soon assign it to somebody else.'

Marsden was doing no more than play games, Beresford thought, feeling his right hand clenching into a fist.

'Of course Crane is up to it,' he said. 'We've got a couple of sniffer dogs that would be up to it, with a bit of training. It's no more than clerical drudgery, and it's a wilful waste of the talents of a good detective.'

'Which one do you think you are?' Marsden asked. 'My guess would be Eric Clapton.'

'I don't know what you're talking about,' Beresford said.

'Or maybe you don't think your team is Cream at all. Maybe you think you're Crosby, Stills, Nash and Young – or some other supergroup. But let me tell you this, Inspector Beresford – there are officers in this division (and I'm one of them), who are sick to death of you and the rest of Chief Inspector Polak's team strutting around like you're cocks of the walk.'

Though he knew his hand was clenched into a fist, Beresford was not even aware he'd taken a swing at the other man before he felt it make contact with Marsden's jaw. It seemed to come as a surprise to Marsden, too, but if his mind didn't know what was happening, his body recognized the situation immediately, and responded by crashing backwards onto the ground.

You're out of control again, Colin, said the voice in his head. And this time – you bloody fool – you're out of control with a *policeman*!

Maybe he was a bloody fool – but he didn't care. His body swollen with rage, he looked down at the fallen man, and said, 'Get up, you bastard.'

'Have you gone crazy?' Marsden asked, staying where he had fallen, but gently probing his jaw with his left hand. 'Don't you know that could cost you your job?'

'My boss is the best bobby in Central Lancs – and she's fighting for her life,' Beresford said. 'She's entitled to some respect.'

'Do you want to help me back up to my feet?' Marsden asked, holding out his hand.

Beresford hesitated for a second, then took the hand and pulled Marsden up.

Marsden looked around him.

'Do you think there's a possibility that anybody saw what just happened?' he asked.

'You don't need witnesses,' the bloody fool who had once been DI Beresford said. 'I'm not the least bit sorry for what I just did, and if you haul me up in front of the top brass, I'll not deny it.'

'You've got it arse over backwards,' Marsden told him. 'I'd only report you if there *were* witnesses – because I'd really have no choice. So do you think anybody saw what went down?'

'No.'

'Then I won't report you.'

'*Why* won't you report me?'

'Partly because you're right – your boss is a good detective, if a bit too flashy for my taste, and I had no right to refer to her in the way I did.'

'And what's the other reason?' Beresford asked.

'That doesn't matter.'

'The other reason is that you'd be too embarrassed that you didn't see the punch coming,' Beresford guessed, 'and that when I landed it, it was enough to knock you down.'

Marsden looked uncomfortable. 'If you brag to anybody else about this, all bets are off,' he said.

'I won't tell anybody,' Beresford promised. He stood to one side and held his arms out. 'Do you want to take a free swing at me?'

Marsden shook his head. 'I'm not going to sink to your level – but neither am I going to stand by and watch your team steal all the glory from this investigation. Is that clear, DI Beresford?'

'We've never been ones to chase after glory,' Beresford said sincerely.

'Of course you haven't,' Marsden replied, with a sneer.

Then he turned, and started to walk back across the car park.

Beresford – for some reason he couldn't quite explain – found he was rubbing his own jaw.

Last night it had been some drinker in a pub, this morning it had been a detective inspector, he thought.

Who knew what might happen in the afternoon?

Maybe he'd headbutt the chief constable!

As he rode out of Whitebridge, he could feel the tears streaming down his face, behind his visor.

What was he crying for? he wondered.

It certainly wasn't for the girl. It wasn't even really for himself.

No, it was for the bike, which, even now, was faithfully carrying him to the site of what would be its own destruction.

He loved that bike. He'd spent two years saving up for it – denying himself all the treats all his friends took for granted; risking the occasional bit of petty thieving, if he thought it might put a few bob in the bike fund.

Even then, he'd not had enough money to buy it in the normal way – the proper way – but he'd wanted it so badly that he'd been willing to take his chances and had gone the dodgy route instead.

He had left the town behind him, and now was crossing the empty moors. On any other occasion, he would have opened the bike up – let it show what it could really do – but it was bad taste to show off in a funeral cortège, even a unitary one without witnesses, and so he kept to a sombre speed.

If he hadn't lost his temper with the girl, she would still be alive now, he told himself. If he hadn't lost his temper with the girl, he wouldn't now be taking his bike on its last ever ride.

As he rode past the bus stop for the Moorland Bus Company, he checked his watch. He still had time to do what he needed to do, and then get back to this stop in time to catch the afternoon service back into Whitebridge, he thought, but it was going to be tight.

A track branched off the main road to the left, and he took it. The track had a rough surface, made worse by the quarry lorries which had once ploughed it up, and at any other time, he would have worried about what it was doing to his bike's tyres. Now, of course, it didn't matter, because all the bike had to do was to carry him for another quarter of a mile.

He stopped the bike at the lip of the quarry, and looked down at the steep slope which led to the bottom of it. A lake had formed in the abandoned workings, and though he didn't know how deep it was, he was sure it was deep enough.

He felt a sudden impulse to stay on the bike – to ride it down the steep slope and into the dark water. But the impulse soon passed, because although he deeply regretted what he had done, he still did not regret it enough to want to pay with his own life.

He dismounted, wheeled the bike to the edge, and gave it a gentle push.

For perhaps the first quarter of its journey, it stayed upright. Then it hit a rock, the front wheel buckled, and it was over. That didn't matter. As a result of the momentum it had already achieved, and the gradient it found itself on, it continued moving – bouncing into the air, crashing on the ground, then bouncing again – until it hit the lake with a resounding splash, and sank from view.

He took off his helmet – because why would he need it now? – and threw it after the bike.

Bounce, bounce, bounce . . . splash.

He turned, and saw the hiker – bobble hat on his head, rucksack on his back, stout stick in his hand – looking at him.

Are you crazy? the man's expression seemed to be asking. That was a good bike – a very good bike – and you've destroyed it!

If he'd kept his helmet on, the hiker would have had no idea what he looked like.

But you didn't do that, did you? he asked himself. Oh no – you had to go for the grand gesture; you had to leave yourself open to being fingered.

He wondered what to do next.

Should he try to explain?

'It looked in good nick, but it was falling to pieces, really.'

Should he threaten?

'If you tell anybody what you've seen, I'll hunt you down wherever you are. I promise you that.'

Or should he, perhaps, make absolutely certain that the man never told anybody anything that he'd seen?

It would be very easily done, he thought. The man was clearly weaker than he was. He was middle-aged, and so, presumably had already had the best that life had to offer him, which was why his idea of fun now seemed to be a lonely walk across a bleak moor.

It would probably be doing him a favour to end his life now. It would probably . . .

'Tipping a good bike into a quarry – are you soft in the head, lad?' the hiker asked.

The words had the instant effect of driving any crazy notions out of his mind – of driving *any* notions out of his mind, if truth be told.

He turned, and jogged back down the track.

When the bus came, the driver gave him a slightly strange look, but said nothing, and as he sank back into his seat, he felt a sense of relief.

It had cost him his beloved bike, he told himself – but he had probably got away with it.

SIX

When Cynthia Broadbent had entered the teaching profession, just after the war, she'd had visions of herself as a headmistress of a prestigious school – of being an educator whose sage pronouncements would be regularly reported in the *Times Educational Supplement*. It had taken her perhaps two years working at the chalk face to realize that she did not have the determination, charisma, gravitas or ruthlessness necessary to become an effective leader, and thereafter she had settled for slowly climbing the educational ladder, so that now, a few years from retirement, she had finally been promoted to second deputy head.

She had known other women who, on being appointed to similar positions, had become martinets, striding extravagantly and loudly along the school corridors as if they had taken the head of the SS as their role model. She, in contrast, had chosen a much quieter, softer approach to her work – more Albert Schweitzer than Heinrich Himmler.

The position suited her, and seemed likely to continue to do so into the next decade, at which point she would be old enough to claim her pension. When that time arrived, she would buy a cottage by the seaside with her friend, Miss Tweedsmuir, who, though a teetotaller, had been working as a bookkeeper at the local brewery for over twenty years, and if their new seaside neighbours decided to regard the two late-middle-aged women living together as a pair of rampant lesbians, well, that was their business.

This lunchtime, she had just been down to the main gate to shoo away the reporters – there weren't many, most had had the decency to stay away. Now, walking back across the playground, she considered the impact the murder might have on the school community.

The children were bound to be somewhat upset, of course, but nowhere near as upset as if someone else – say, Louisa Paniatowski – had been killed.

Louisa involved herself wholeheartedly in the life of the school. Everybody knew her, and everybody liked her. Mary, on the other hand, had belonged to that small band of pupils who seemed to be *in* the school, but not *of* it. And it was wrong to call them a band, Miss Broadbent thought, because what defined a band was that they stuck together, and these children stuck to nobody at all – were, in fact, solitary islands floating in a sea of friendships and alliances.

It was as she was approaching the bike sheds that Miss Broadbent noticed the girl wearing the prefect's badge.

Now, for goodness sake, what was she doing there? Miss Broadbent wondered – and walking over to the girl, she asked just that question.

'It's my turn to be on dinner duty, miss,' Louisa Paniatowski said, in her responsible prefect-voice. 'It's down on the rota.'

'Well, yes, that may well be the case, but given the circumstances, surely someone else—'

'Please don't send me home, miss,' Louisa pleaded, the prefect-voice having quite disappeared, and tears forming at the corners of her eyes.

'I was just thinking of your little brothers,' Miss Broadbent said, suddenly feeling inadequate to deal with the situation.

'As Elena's pointed out—'

'Who is Elena?'

'She's a Spanish girl we employ. She's sort of part-house keeper, part-child minder.'

'I see.'

'Anyway, as she says, she can make a much better job of looking after the twins than I could, because she's a lot less personally involved.'

'Then perhaps you could go and sit with your mother?' Miss Broadbent suggested, still keeping her head above water in the sea of confusion which had engulfed her – but only just.

'There's only so much time that I can spend with Mum before I start wanting to go and find a roof to throw myself off,' Louisa said.

'Now you mustn't talk like that, my dear,' Miss Broadbent said, as confusion turned seamlessly into panic.

'That's just a bit of black Northern humour, miss,' Louisa said, with a weak grin. 'I don't expect I'd really kill myself. Apart from anything else, we're Catholic – and if Mum *did* die, the babies would need me more than ever. All I really meant was, it's comforting to be here, if only for a little while – doing the job I know how to do, seeing what I expect to see.'

Miss Broadbent could never remember patting a pupil on the shoulder before, but she patted Louisa now.

'You do what you need to do, my dear,' she said, 'and if you ever need a shoulder to cry on, you know where my office is.'

It wasn't that Colin Beresford didn't mind being alone, but rather that he had had to, of necessity, get used to it. For years, while caring for his mother (who had been struck down with early-onset Alzheimer's), he had spent most of his evenings alone, even though she had often been in the room with him. And later, after she had died and he had set about acquiring his reputation as *Shagger*

Beresford, he had made a conscious choice to be alone, especially after sex, because to linger in a temporary partner's bed too long would, it seemed to him, hint at a commitment he was simply not prepared to make.

The one place he really didn't like being alone, he had only just discovered, was in the police canteen. Canteen culture was, by its very essence, a matey culture, and it was normal to be there with at least one other member of the team, but Meadows was out with DS Higgins, Crane was in the technology room, and Monika . . . Monika was fighting (and who could say just how successfully) for her life.

He could, he supposed, have joined the other team – the *parallel* team, which saw his own team's success as nothing more than a quest for glory, and wrote off as pure bloody luck all the hard work, good leadership and occasional sliver of pure bloody inspiration which often brought about a successful result – but he suspected he wouldn't be welcome, and so he sat alone, sipping industrial strength tea from a big white mug which felt almost heavy enough to serve as the proverbial blunt instrument.

He felt his spirits rise when he saw Jack Crane enter the canteen, but his pleasure quickly changed gear, sliding into curiosity, when he saw the look on the young detective constable's face.

'There's something you need to see at once, sir,' Crane said, without preamble.

'On the CCTV tapes?'

'Yes.'

'And what's the urgency?'

'I'm supposed to report to DI Marsden the moment I uncover anything that might be of significance.'

'And . . .?'

'I think what I've found might be a major lead, and I don't want it to be sucked into Marsden's vortex before you've had a chance to look at it.'

'Come again?' Beresford said.

'We need to share the lead – because it's *our* boss who's lying in that hospital, and that makes the whole investigation *our* business.'

'You're right, Jack,' Beresford agreed. 'You're bloody spot on.'

*   *   *

The technology room could more accurately have been called the technology cupboard, and even with just the two of them there, it felt very crowded.

'I know the only reason Marsden gave me this job was to make it clear that, as members of the boss's team, we're expected to do all the donkey work,' Crane said, as he threaded the tape around the spool, 'but it's worked out very well, because if any other bobby had been put on the job, we'd still be hours away from getting this information.'

He sounded like he was bragging, Beresford thought. But he probably wasn't. As far as he could tell, Crane *never* bragged, maybe because the young detective constable had so much self-confidence that he didn't feel the need to.

'So why did you get to it quicker than anybody else would have done?' Beresford asked.

'Most of the bobbies that I've come across are methodical to the point of plodding—' Crane began.

'Got anybody in particular in mind?' Beresford asked.

'Oh, not you, sir,' Crane said, perhaps just a little *too* hastily. 'Anyway, what they tend to do is start at the beginning, work their way through to the end, and then stop.'

'And you don't?'

'No, I'm a university boy – as everyone round here suddenly seems to get malicious pleasure in reminding me – and I approach a job the way I used to approach my studies, which is by getting an overview first, and then homing in on what seems particularly significant.'

'Right, that's the commercial over and done with ⌐ now let's see the result,' Beresford said.

Crane grinned, awkwardly. 'Sorry, I must have sounded like a bit of a knob,' he said. 'Anyway, take a look at this.'

Crane pressed the fast forward button. Beresford watched as coaches passed through the West Gate at breakneck speed, followed by cars which seemed to be going even faster. Then they reached the point in the tape that Crane had been looking for, and he pressed the freeze button.

'What do you see?' he asked.

Beresford saw a Honda 250cc motorbike. The driver was wearing a full-face crash helmet, but from his general shape, he was almost definitely male. The passenger also had a full-face helmet, and was wearing a skirt, holding it down at the front with one hand.

'Could that be Mary Green?' Crane asked.

'It's possible. She's wearing a skirt and Mary was wearing a skirt, but looking at her from that angle – and seeing it in black-and-white – I wouldn't like to say if it's the same skirt or not.'

Crane did not seem the least discouraged. 'What do you make of the box strapped to the back luggage rack?' he asked.

'It looks like a wicker basket,' Beresford said. 'I'd guess it was a picnic hamper.'

'Me, too,' Crane said. 'So we've got these two young people intending to spend a pleasant day in each other's company. Agreed?'

'It seems likely,' Beresford admitted.

'Then just wait till you see the next bit,' Crane said, hitting the fast forward button again.

When Crane stopped the tape again, Beresford glanced at the clock at the bottom of the screen, and saw that just over an hour had passed.

What he was looking at now was a Honda 250cc motorbike, and it was exiting the park.

'It looks like the same bike to me,' he said to Crane. 'Is it?'

Crane nodded. 'Unless it's changed number plates with another motorbike inside the park, then yes, it is.'

'It's looking more and more likely that the girl was Mary Green, and if we can find that picnic hamper somewhere in the woods, we can be almost certain it was her,' Beresford said. 'So what do you think happened once they were in there? Did they have an argument?'

'I don't think so,' Crane said. 'If you have a row with someone – and kill them in a fit of rage – you don't then hang about long enough to wash out your victim's vagina with tea.'

'So you're saying the murder was planned in advance, and the killer was using the idea of a picnic as bait?'

'Essentially, yes,' Crane agreed.

'So he didn't panic at all?'

'No, I don't think he did. I still believe it was a ritual killing, and there's never any panic in a ritual killing, because the killer believes – *has to* believe – that he's doing no less than obeying the laws of the universe, and so, obviously, the universe has to be on his side.'

'Or at least that's what he tells himself before he stabs the knife or swings his hammer, but once he sees blood spurt out or hears bones crunching, he can sometimes lose it – and that's what I think happened here,' Beresford said.

'What have I missed?' Crane wondered.

'He left the picnic hamper behind,' Beresford said. 'That hamper probably contains any number of clues which will lead us to him, and if he'd thought about it, he'd have realized that – but he *didn't* think about it, because the only thought he actually had was to get away.'

'Unless he's more cunning than we think, and leaving the hamper behind was no more than a ploy to mislead us,' Crane said. 'Or – and here's another possibility – the ritual compelled him to leave the hamper behind.'

'You're giving me a headache,' Beresford groaned. 'And you know, when you stop to think about it, you realize that all this speculation is just a waste of time, because we've got the bike's number, which means that we'll soon have the bike's owner, and when we have him, we can ask *him* what the truth is.'

Louisa had told Miss Broadbent that there was some comfort to be found in seeing what she expected to see, but now she was learning that there was some comfort – no, not comfort, but rather, diversion or distraction – to be found in seeing what she'd *never* expected to see.

What had sparked her curiosity was a meeting – and it simply couldn't be called anything else *but* a meeting – that was taking place near the edge of the bike sheds.

There were two things which made it noteworthy – three, if you took into account that, unlike most of the kids who congregated around the bike sheds, none of the participants seemed interested in having a furtive, guilty smoke.

The first of these noteworthy things was that one of the four girls involved was Jennifer Black.

Though Jennifer was a couple of years younger than Louisa, they were both members of Fielden House, and Louisa, who considered it part of her duties as house captain to take an interest in other house members, had been making a note of her behaviour for some time.

Jennifer, it seemed to her, was one of the least sociable girls she had ever met – on a par, she would estimate, with poor Mary Green. She appeared to have no friends and no interests. She would attend a house function without complaint if it was compulsory, but if it wasn't, she wouldn't go within a mile of it. Louisa got the general impression from her teachers (and it was only a *general* impression, because even though she was the most active house captain they could ever remember dealing with, she was still a pupil, so you could only tell her so much) that Jennifer was getting by in her studies, but could have done much better with just a little effort.

Thus, it was strange that this veteran non-participant – this professional opt-outer – should now be engaged in conversation with three other girls.

And that was the second strange thing – none of the girls were the same age as Jennifer!

The youngest, Louisa guessed, was a first year, which would make her going on twelve. The other two were either third years or fourth years. By all the social codes which operated in this school – and had operated in all other schools, since the beginnings of time – these four girls should be having nothing to do with each other. And yet here they were, involved in a deep – almost intense – discussion, which seemed to have been going on for several minutes.

Maybe she should find out what was going on, Louisa thought. It could even be argued that it was her duty to do just that – and if, by being dutiful, she satisfied her own curiosity, well, that was just a handy bonus.

But then, just as she was about to approach them, someone else did – a tall boy in a yellow jumper and blue jeans.

Really, if he was going to be in school at all, he should be in uniform, Louisa thought.

And then she realized how absurd she was being. The boy had just lost his sister – and unlike the case of her mum, there wasn't even the slightest chance of Mary ever coming back.

So did it really matter if he ignored regulations?

Of course not!

He could have turned up naked for all she cared – except that might have frightened some of the younger girls!

John knelt down, so that his own eyes were at the level of those of the smaller girls, and began talking in what was plainly an earnest fashion. But what was really interesting to Louisa – what was bloody amazing, as a matter of fact – was the effect his words seemed to be having on them.

The tension drained from their faces, a smile came to their lips, and they almost glowed with happiness.

Now what was that all about?

The house on Sebastopol Street was a mirror image of the one on Balaclava Street, even down to its navy blue front door and daffodil and snowdrop curtains, but when DS Higgins knocked on the door, no worried-looking, middle-aged woman in a floral pinafore came to answer it.

Instead, a much older woman's voice called out, 'Who is it?'

'It's the police, Mrs Brown,' Higgins said. 'DS Higgins and DS Meadows. We'd like a word with you, if you don't mind.'

'The door's kept on the latch in the daytime,' the woman said. 'You only have to push.'

They stepped into the hallway. The parlour door was open, and inside they could see a bed with a frail-looking woman – who could have been anything from seventy to ninety – lying in it.

'I'm in here,' the woman said unnecessarily.

Higgins and Meadows entered the room, and positioned them-selves at the foot of the bed. Higgins produced his warrant card, though, for all the attention the woman in the bed paid to it, he might as well not have bothered.

'Have you come to ask me about poor little Mary Green?' the old woman asked.

'So you do know she's been murdered?' Higgins said, in a tone that was not *quite* accusatory.

'Yes,' the old woman said, 'my morning home help, Mrs Goodman, told me. It was a terrible shock, of course.'

'Your *morning* home help?' Higgins repeated, as if he were expecting some kind of trick.

'I have three,' the old woman explained. 'One comes in the morning, another, Mrs Holiday, comes in the afternoon, and, in the evening, it's Miss Soper. They each stay for about half an hour. It's how I survive.' A look of self-pity flooded her face for a second, then was gone. 'I shouldn't complain,' she continued. 'I should be grateful for what I have.'

'So your home helps look after you during the week, and Mary looks after you – looked after you – at the weekend?' Higgins asked.

'That's right.'

'And when was the last time you actually saw Mary, Mrs Brown?' Higgins asked.

'Let me think for a minute,' the old woman said. 'It must have been around noon on Sunday. Yes, it was noon, because, as she was leaving, I remember the clock at St Thomas's chiming out the hour.'

'But I thought she stayed here all day on Sunday,' Higgins said. 'I thought she even slept overnight here.'

'So she did, normally,' the old woman agreed. 'But this Sunday, she said she wanted to meet a friend, and asked if I'd mind.'

'That's just typical of the young, these days, isn't it?' Higgins asked. 'They have absolutely no consideration for others.'

I know what you're doing, Meadows thought – you're basing your approach on the assumption that the old will automatically resent the young, and all you need do to set them off on a tirade – which is often more informative than they ever realize – is to press the right button.

Well, there was no disputing that while it might be crude as a method of questioning, it was often very effective.

'I mean, as far as she was concerned, why should she care how you'd manage once she'd gone, as long as she got to meet her friend?' Higgins asked, ramming the approach home.

'Oh no, you mustn't think it was like that at all, because it simply wasn't,' Mrs Brown protested. 'To be honest, she was very tentative about it, and she'd no sooner mentioned the idea than she started to backtrack on herself and say it wasn't important and she'd stay with me. It was all I could do to persuade her that I could manage on my own once she'd gone.'

'How *did* you manage?' Meadows asked.

'Oh, I can deal with most things, if I really put my mind to it and take my time,' Mrs Brown said. 'I couldn't make the bed or prepare a meal, of course, but I can go to the toilet without help, and I can wash myself.' She paused for a second, then, managing to look both ashamed and defiant, she continued, 'I can wash most parts of me, anyway.'

'Did Mary often abandon you on a Sunday?' Higgins asked, reluctant to abandon his chosen line of approach, though, so far, it had brought him no results at all.

'Oh no, of course she didn't,' Mrs Brown said. 'In fact, last Sunday was the first time she's ever done it.'

Meadows felt her finely tuned bullshit antennae tingle.

First time she'd ever done it?

Like hell it was!

'What can you tell me about this friend of hers that she was meeting?' Higgins said.

'Well, nothing, really,' Mrs Brown said.

Another lie, Meadows thought.

'But it was a *boyfriend*, wasn't it?'

'I don't know,' Mrs Brown said.

'You don't *know*?'

'I didn't think to ask.'

'I find that very strange,' Higgins mused. 'If I was in your situation, I think my natural curiosity would have forced me to ask.'

'But you're not in my situation, are you?' the old woman asked. 'And anyway, I was brought up to consider minding your own business as no more than good manners.'

Higgins scowled – and the scowl deepened when he saw that Meadows was grinning.

'Did he pick Mary up from here on Sunday, Mrs Brown?' the detective sergeant asked.

'No, he . . .' the old woman began. Then she realized her mistake, and was silent for several seconds before saying, 'Mary went off to meet this friend of hers somewhere else.'

'And where did they go?'

'It must have been to that big house, mustn't it, since that's where they found her body?'

'Everybody I've talked to tells me she was a lovely girl,' Higgins said, abandoning his 'teenagers are shit' approach in favour of something much more benevolent.

'She was,' Mrs Brown agreed. 'She was *such* a lovely girl.'

'And I'm sure that you'd like to see her killer brought to justice, wouldn't you?'

'Yes.'

'So why don't you help us, Mrs Brown? Why don't you tell us what you know about this boyfriend of hers?'

'I don't know anything,' Mrs Brown said, turning to Meadows for help. 'I'm an old woman. I haven't left this house for years.'

Meadows had been looking around the room. There was no Chinese girl or flying ducks, but there was a painting of a child with apple cheeks and almost grotesquely large eyes, and on the shelf which hung over the bed there were three Toby jugs of various sizes, so it was likely that Hitchcock would have been as happy with this set as he'd have been with the Greens' front parlour.

'I imagine you spend most of the day in bed, don't you, Mrs Brown?' she asked, sympathetically.

'Yes, I do,' the old woman agreed, clearly grateful to have the focus shifted from Mary Green to her own poor health. 'There's not much choice in the matter. It's the price that you pay for getting old – as you'll find out yourself, eventually.'

Meadows grinned. 'If I live that long,' she said.

The old woman returned the grin with a weak smile. 'Well, you certainly won't find out if you *don't* live that long,' she said.

'It must get very boring for you, just lying there, with no one to talk to,' Meadows said, laying on the sympathy with a trowel.

'It does,' the old woman agreed.

'Still, I expect television helps,' Meadows said artlessly. She looked around the room. 'I don't see your TV, Mrs Brown. Is it in the kitchen?'

'No,' Mrs Brown said, speaking cautiously now, as if she had started to suspect that the woman she'd embraced as an ally was about to turn out to be no friend at all.

'So where is your television?' Meadows asked, still guileless.

'I don't have one,' the old woman told her.

'And why is that?'

'Televisions cost a lot of money,' the old woman said. 'I'm only a poor pensioner.'

Meadows beamed with obvious delight. 'Well, this is your lucky day, Mrs Brown,' she said.

'What do you mean?'

'A girlfriend of mine has just emigrated to Australia, and she's left her television with me. But I already have one, you see, so I've been wondering what to do with it. And now I know – I'll bring it round here for you, Mrs Brown.'

'I couldn't afford the licence fee,' Mrs Brown said.

'Oh, don't you go worrying your head about that,' Meadows said airily. 'I'll have a whip-round at the station. No one will begrudge putting a few bob in the hat to help an old lady.'

'I don't want it,' Mrs Brown said, starting to sound hostile. 'I can't be doing with it.'

And she wasn't *just* hostile, Meadows thought, there was an element of fear in there, too – the old woman was frightened at even the *idea* of having a television in her house.

Meadows laughed, though neither of the others had any idea what she had found funny.

'You got a bit cross with me, then, didn't you, Mrs Brown?' she asked.

'I suppose I did, a little,' the old woman agreed.

'And when you did, your accent changed,' Meadows said. 'You could easily have passed as a native up to that point, but you're not from round here at all, are you?'

'Well, no,' the old woman admitted.

'So where are you from originally? I'd guess you come from Somerset. Am I right?'

'Yes,' the old woman said, with reluctance.

'But I expect you've lived here a long time, have you?'

'Quite a while.'

'Now doesn't that just cover a multitude of sins?' Meadows asked, laughing again to show she wasn't being serious. 'How long – exactly – have you lived here, Mrs Brown?'

'It must be five years.'

'And you came here directly from Somerset?'

'Yes.'

'You're a widow, I take it.'

'Yes.'

'And was your husband alive when you made the move?'

'No, he'd already passed on.'

Meadows clicked her tongue sympathetically. 'How brave of

you to make the move entirely on your own,' she said. 'Your arthritis – it is arthritis you've got, isn't it?'

'Yes.'

'Your arthritis must have come on you very suddenly, then – say, in the last two or three years – mustn't it?'

It was plain from the look on the old woman's face that she was contemplating agreeing with Meadows, but then seemed to decide it would be safer to stick to the truth and said, 'No, it wasn't the last two or three years – I've been suffering from it for much longer than that.'

'Well, I do call that *extra* brave of you, moving to somewhere new – somewhere a couple of hundred miles from home – when you *already* had arthritis. Still, I assume you must already have had lots of friends in Whitebridge before you even arrived.'

Again, there was the temptation to agree, and once more Mrs Brown decided it was wiser not to.

'I didn't know anybody from around here,' she admitted.

'Oh,' Meadows said, sounding both puzzled and troubled. 'So what made you move?'

'I felt like a change.'

'And fortunately, you'd no sooner arrived than Mary Green was knocking on your door and offering to look after you when the home helps couldn't,' Meadows said brightly.

'No.'

'No?'

'It wasn't Mary in those days. It was another girl.'

'And what was her name?'

'I can't remember.'

'Please try, just for me.'

'I'm an old woman, and I can't remember.'

'Doesn't really matter,' Meadows said, in an almost carefree manner. 'Can you remember how the girls – Mary and the one before her – found out about you? Was it through the social services department? Or was it some other organization – like the Salvation Army?'

'I want you both to leave,' the old woman said with sudden, surprising firmness.

'If I've done something to offend you, then I'm most terribly sorry, but you can't blame me for being curious, can you?' Meadows asked.

'I want you to leave,' the old woman repeated. 'I want you to leave right now.'

'I can't believe what just happened in there,' Higgins said, once they were out on the street again. 'There was I, trying to talk to a witness who may have had valuable information, and you got us thrown out.'

'You've not missed anything,' Meadows said. 'If she did have any valuable information, she certainly wasn't about to share it with you.'

'I don't even know where you were hoping to go with that odd line of questioning,' Higgins complained. 'You don't think the old woman killed Mary Green, do you?'

'No, of course I don't,' Meadows said, 'but you must surely have noticed that not only are Mr and Mrs Green and Mrs Brown all weird, but they're weird in more or less the same way.'

'The fact that they haven't got televisions, and seem to share a poor taste in interior decoration, doesn't mean that any of them had anything to do with the murder, does it?' Higgins asked.

'No, it doesn't,' Meadows agreed, 'but the more we understand where Mary Green was coming from, the greater our chances of working out how she ended up as she did.'

'That's a bit deep for a hardworking, straightforward bobby like me,' Higgins said. 'Do you want to go back to headquarters now?'

'You can, if you like,' Meadows said easily.

'And what about you?'

'I think I should go and have a talk to this Roger Smith, who John Green claims he was playing Diplomacy with all day yesterday, but there's no reason why you should come along and waste the time of two detective sergeants.'

And that was probably how it started with Paniatowski's team, Higgins thought. They announced, quite casually, that they were off to follow a lead which they didn't think was going to lead them anywhere, and before you knew it, they'd got the case solved and were hogging all the glory.

'I think I'll come with you,' Higgins said.

Meadows shrugged. 'Please yourself.'

She sounded indifferent – but was that any more than pretence?

Higgins glanced down at his watch. 'Do you think your Mr Smith will be at home at this time of day?' he asked.

'If my theory's correct, he's almost bound to be,' Meadows said, enigmatically.

She is back in the woods again. She still doesn't know why she's there – or why it's important that she knows *why she's there – but she knows it does matter, and that's progress of a sort.*

It's not the same woods that she was in the last time. It's not a Polish forest at all, but a quintessentially English wood. And since she knows the word quintessentially, she must be quite old, because it's certainly not a word that the young Monika – light enough and small enough to be lifted through the air and share a saddle with her father – would ever have known.

It had been light in the Polish woods – shafts of sunlight filtered magically through the trees, and it was not difficult to believe that, hidden just out of sight, wood nymphs were going about their fairy business.

These woods are dark – the natural home of trolls and goblins – and somewhere in the distance there is the sound of the sort of music which, while it may not actually belong to the devil, is certainly devoid of holiness.

Suddenly, she comes across two men – dirty, smelly men – squatting down in a clearing, counting out money.

Then, before she knows what is happening, these two men are holding her down, pressing her into the ground and a third – equally repulsive – is entering her with brutal disregard.

She can feel the man thrusting away inside her, but she is also outside her own body, observing the process at a distance.

This is when it happened, she tells herself – this is when Philip and Thomas were conceived.

She feels both shame and horror, and yet the overwhelming feeling is one of disappointment.

She is not here to relive the rape, any more than she had been in the forest to see her dead father. These are things of the past, and her purpose in being there now is very much to do with the present.

Yet she still has no idea what that purpose is.

SEVEN

Roger Smith – the supposed Diplomacy player – lived in Inkerman Street, which was about midway between Balaclava Street and Sebastopol Street. Like the Greens and Mrs Brown, he lived in a terraced house, and like them, he had a front door that was painted navy blue.

'Doesn't that strike you as odd?' Meadows asked, as they stood on the pavement outside the house.

'Doesn't what strike me as odd?' Higgins said.

'That all the houses we've visited have front doors of exactly the same colour?'

Higgins laughed.

'What's so funny?' Meadows wondered.

'There's an old joke about the lady researcher from London who comes to find what life "up north" is like,' Higgins said. 'Anyway, she's walking down this back alley, and she sees this tiny little house, so she knocks on the door. "Yes?" says a girl's voice from inside. "Will you let me in?" the researcher asks. "I can't," the girl says, "I'm busy." So the researcher asks if she can ask the questions through the door, and the girl says that will be all right. "How many people live in your house?" the researcher asks. "There's me, me mam, me dad, and me three sisters," the girl says. The researcher steps to one side, so she can get a better look at the house. It can't be more than four feet wide and ten feet deep, yet somehow, six people manage to live in it. "And me granny, and me granddad, and me auntie," the girl continues. Ten people – six of them grown-ups. It doesn't seem possible. Then the researcher feels a tap on her shoulder, and when she turns round she finds herself facing a woman who not only looks angry, but has her hands on her hips – which, as you might realize, is a sign that she's really pissed off. "If you don't mind," this woman says, "I'd like you to explain exactly what you think you're doing loitering in front of our lavatory".' DS Higgins chuckled again. 'It wasn't where they lived, you see, love – it was only their shit house.'

'And the point of that story is that I'm an off-comer who has no idea how things are done in Whitebridge?' Meadows asked.

'Well, exactly,' Higgins agreed. 'Of course, it's always possible the front doors are painted blue to identify the people inside as members of a wife-swapping ring, but the idea of sticking my thing into Mrs Green's withered old—'

'Get to the point,' Meadows snapped.

'How dare you talk to me like that!' Higgins said. 'I'm the senior sergeant here, and I demand my right to be treated with the proper respect.'

Except that it didn't quite come out like that.

Because though those were the words that were formed in his mind, somewhere between there and his mouth, his instinct stepped in and warned him that Meadows wouldn't like it, and that his heart, stomach and spleen were quite worried about how she might react.

So that when the message did finally emerge, what Higgins said on behalf of his various body parts was, 'Keep your shirt on, DS Meadows – I'm getting round to it.'

'No hurry,' Meadows said, with all the sarcasm inherent in native Whitebridge wit.

'One of this town's biggest industries is paint,' Higgins explained. 'Monarch paints have a worldwide reputation for quality – but despite how fresh the paintwork looks in this town, not much of it is sold here.'

'Because it's knocked off,' Meadows guessed.

'Because it's knocked off,' Higgins agreed. 'And as soon as it is knocked off, you'll find some wide boy selling it from door to door, at bargain prices. Only you don't have a choice of colours, you take whatever colour has been "liberated", so some years, everybody's using claret, and other years it's navy blue.'

'Well, it was worth a shot, at least,' Meadows said philosophically. She knocked on the navy blue front door. 'Let's see what our Mr Smith has to say for himself.'

The man who answered her knock was five feet ten inches tall, and around forty-five years old. Meadows did not judge men by their looks – it was their ability to be moderately cruel which drew her to them – but she had to concede that Smith was quite a handsome man.

'Yes?' he said.

'Oh, come on now, Mr Smith, don't pretend to be taken so completely by surprise – you must have been expecting our call!' Meadows said, holding up her warrant card.

'Actually, I *wasn't* expecting your call,' Smith said. 'Since I didn't know Mary Green, I could see no reason for you making one. As a matter of fact, I still can't.'

'You don't know Mary Green, but you know her brother, John,' Meadows said.

'Yes, that's true enough,' Smith conceded.

'You wouldn't mind if we came inside for a few minutes, would you, sir?' Higgins asked.

'As a matter of fact I would mind,' Smith told him. 'I've got a great deal to get through today, and since I'm satisfied in my own mind that I can't be of any real help to you—'

'We have reason to believe these premises are being used for immoral purposes,' Higgins said.

'How dare you?' Smith demanded, proving, by the expression on his face, that he did outrage extremely well. 'On what basis would you ever think of making such a statement?'

Higgins shrugged. 'You spent last Sunday cloistered with three young men,' he said. 'You really should be able to work out what I'm basing my suspicions on for yourself.'

'That was perfectly innocent,' Smith protested, 'we were playing Diplomacy.'

'Maybe you were, but what I've learned is that if you want to get a search warrant for somebody's house, you've only to whisper the word "pervert" to the issuing magistrate.' Higgins shook his head sagely. 'Magistrates are very conventional people, and they really *don't* like perverts, you know.'

'Do you actually think I'm a pervert?' Smith asked.

'I don't know,' Higgins admitted. 'I'm sort of standing on the borderline at the moment – teetering on a knife edge, as you might say. I think it's more than possible that you could persuade me you're not a pervert, but if you haven't got the time . . .'

'I suppose you'd better come in,' Smith said, bowing to the inevitable.

The first thing they noticed as they stepped into the hallway was a large red suitcase.

'Are you planning to go away, Mr Smith?' Meadows asked.

'Yes, my mother's not well, but it's not serious, and I only expect to be away for a few days,' Smith said.

'It's a big suitcase for a few days.'

'It's the only one I own – I don't travel much.'

Smith turned the handle on the parlour door, and pushed the door open. 'Go inside. I'll make some tea.'

'That's all right, sir, we don't want any tea,' Meadows said.

'But I do,' Smith told her.

As they entered their third parlour of the day, Meadows had a pretty good idea of what to expect, and was not disappointed. In this parlour, the pictures on the walls were of boxers, and the ornaments on the mantelpiece were racing cars, but once again, this seemed like a film set (and a rather old-fashioned one) rather than being somewhere that someone actually lived. But here, at least, there was one difference – unlike the Greens and Mrs Brown, Mr Smith actually had a television set.

Smith returned with the tea tray. He looked first at Meadows, then around the room, and finally back at Meadows again.

He didn't really want tea at all, Meadows thought, with a sudden burst of insight. What he wanted to do was to give us the opportunity to see how normal his home is.

'Take a seat,' Smith said.

'We'd prefer to stand, sir,' Higgins said. 'Keeps the whole business on an official footing, if you know what I mean.'

'Very well,' Smith said, discarding the tea tray – which was no longer of use to anyone, now it had served its purpose – on a low occasional table.

'So you say that John Green and two other boys were playing Diplomacy in here all day Sunday,' Higgins said.

'That's right.'

'And no one ever left the house at all.'

'That's correct.'

'Not even to eat?'

'No. I made us a big plate of sandwiches before the game began, but it all got so exciting that half of them were still left at the end.'

It was one of those little details, Meadows thought, that people insert into their conversation because they think it gives it an air of authenticity. Sometimes that worked, and sometimes it didn't. This time, it definitely didn't work for her.

'Who won in the end?' Higgins asked casually.

It was still remotely possible that Smith was telling the truth, Meadows thought, but if he wasn't, he certainly wasn't going to be tripped up by as simple a trick as that.

'Nobody won,' Smith said. 'The game wasn't completed. We were going to finish it off next week, but now that John's sister has been murdered, I expect that will never happen.'

'What I don't understand is why you don't play with men of your own age,' Higgins said.

'If I knew any men of my own age who wanted to play the game, then I would gladly play with them,' Smith said. 'What you seem to fail to understand, sergeant, is that the players are not important to me beyond the fact that they are willing to play the game. I'd play with chimpanzees, if they could learn the rules and turned out to be worthy opponents.'

'So you're a fanatic,' Higgins said, smiling.

'I suppose I am,' Smith agreed, returning the smile.

'But how did you find out the other three were also fanatics?' Higgins said, springing what he fondly imagined to be yet another trap.

'I don't recall saying they *were* fanatics,' Smith countered.

'Surely, if they're prepared to stay here all day Sunday, playing one game, then they must be.'

'I suppose you're right,' Smith agreed, 'but as I've already explained, I tend not to think of my opponents as people at all.'

'Then how *do* you think about them?'

'As threats.'

'That is interesting,' Higgins said. 'Well, that's just about it.' He turned towards the door, then stopped himself. 'Though now I think about it, you still haven't answered the question I asked earlier.'

'And what question might that be?' Smith wondered.

'How did you first make contact with these three lads?' Higgins said.

'Through an advertisement in a gaming magazine,' Smith said.

'Are there such things?' Higgins wondered, looking at Meadows and inviting her to comment.

'There are at least half a dozen I could name, and probably a lot more,' Meadows told him.

Higgins sighed. 'You said you were going away for a few days, Mr Smith,' he said. 'Not too far, I hope?'

'No, just to Skipton.'

'Well, that's not far at all. We'll need the address you're staying at, of course.'

An innocent man would have given his address immediately, Meadows thought, and a guilty man would have refused without a second thought. But there was a class between them – the man who was not quite sure how guilty he was – who would hesitate before agreeing, and that was what Smith did now.

Once he had the address, Higgins seemed willing to leave, but Meadows said, 'I have a few questions of my own, if you don't mind.'

'Do I have to answer them?' Smith asked, playing the all-fellers-together card by addressing the question to Higgins.

'I'd certainly advise you to,' Higgins said, displaying absolutely no sign of either support or sympathy.

Smith sighed. 'All right.'

'Where do you work, Mr Smith?' Meadows asked.

'Is this really relevant?'

'It could be.'

'I'm not actually working at the moment,' Smith said.

'So you're unemployed.'

'I prefer to think of it as resting between periods of employment – a little like an actor.'

'And what do you do for a living when you *are* working, Mr Smith?' Meadows asked.

'I'm a counsellor.'

'And what does that mean exactly?'

'It means that when people have problems in their lives, they come to me and I counsel them.'

'Are you trained?' Meadows asked.

'I'm not sure quite what you mean by that,' Smith said evasively.

'I mean that if I asked you to produce a certificate from an institute of higher education, would you be able to do it?'

'No.'

'So basically, you're unqualified.'

'I have a natural talent for the work, and I have learned much from watching others.'

'So you're sensitive to other people's emotions and concerns?'

'Highly sensitive.'

'Except that when you're playing Diplomacy, your opponents hardly exist as people at all.'

'I have the ability to delineate my work from my pleasure.'

'I wish I could do that,' Meadows said reflectively. 'You say you didn't know Mary Green?'

'That's right – I never met her.'

'How about the parents – Mr and Mrs Green?'

'I don't know them, either.'

'What about Mrs Brown?'

'No, I don't know her.'

He realized his mistake the moment that the words were out of his mouth, but by then it was too late.

'Now that is interesting,' Meadows said. 'If you'd asked me that question, I'm sure I'd have said something like, "Do you mean Mrs Joan Brown who used to be landlady of the Rising Sun, or are you talking about Mrs Gwyneth Brown, the vicar's wife?" But not you! You don't know any Browns.'

'That's right,' Smith agreed, through teeth which were almost clenched. 'I don't know *any* Mrs Browns.'

'How strange, when Brown is such a common name,' Meadows mused. 'And come to think of it, Green's a common name, too.'

'I suppose so.'

'Not to mention "Smith".'

'You really have to go now,' Smith said.

'There are a couple more things—' Meadows began.

'You really have to go now,' Smith repeated.

And he was right. They had nothing on him, and if he wanted them to leave, there was nothing they could do about it.

With three of them in the technology room, there was no room for anyone to move, and so, with some show of reluctance, Colin Beresford had stepped out into the corridor.

That had been ten minutes earlier, and now he was starting to worry that maybe Jack Crane was not presenting the evidence in the right way, and DCI Dixon would dismiss this line of inquiry as a complete waste of time.

And it was vitally important that they catch this feller, he told himself, because somehow the belief had become fixed in his mind that if they *didn't* catch him, Monika would never come out of her coma.

The door opened, and Rhino Dixon squeezed his big frame through the technology room's narrow opening into the corridor.

'He's a smart lad, yon Crane, despite him having got his mind all messed up by going to university,' he said.

'Yes, sir, he is a smart lad,' Beresford said, not *quite* ready to feel relieved yet, but pretty close.

'There's no doubt in my mind that it was Mary Green on that motorcycle, and there's absolutely no doubt that the man who was driving it is our murderer,' Dixon continued.

Beresford felt a sudden (and totally unexpected) wave of doubt wash over him. Yes, he thought that the feller on the bike was the murderer, and yes, he had been praying that Dixon reached the same conclusion. But Rhino's cast-iron certainty unsettled him. Because when you were *so* certain, you ignored anything that didn't fit neatly into your theory – and when that happened, you could get things so very, very wrong.

'Yes, Crane's done a good job,' Dixon continued. 'I'll make sure it's written up in the most glowing possible terms.' He checked his watch. 'Now if I was you, I'd take young Crane out for half a dozen pints of best bitter, if that is, university boys *drink* best bitter.'

'What about the investigation, sir?' Beresford asked.

'What about it?' Dixon asked, putting on a fair show of being completely mystified.

'Well, we need to trace the licence plate, and then we can—'

'Oh, don't you worry about that,' Dixon said. 'That's nowt but coolie work. The real job has already been done, and what's left is no more than a mopping up operation. My team can handle all that, easily enough.'

'With respect, sir, I'd like my team to play a central part in the rest of the investigation, too,' Beresford said.

'Ah, but there's the point,' Dixon asked, his voice hardening a little. 'It's not *your* team at all, is it?'

'Isn't it?' Beresford asked, knocked completely off-kilter by the unexpected nature of the words.

'No, it isn't,' Dixon confirmed. 'It's DCI Paniatowski's team – and right now, she isn't here to command them.'

'I don't see what difference that makes, sir,' Beresford said. 'DCI Paniatowski trained us to operate indep—'

'Of course you don't see what difference it makes,' DCI Dixon interrupted him. 'That's because you're seeing this through an inspector's eyes, looking up – a sort of worm's eye view, if you like – while I'm viewing the whole matter from above, which means I'm able to get everything in perspective.'

That was the biggest load of bollocks he'd heard in a long time, Beresford thought, but it was clear that the DCI wasn't going to budge, so there was no point in arguing.

'Don't worry about it, Colin – we'll get your man for you,' Dixon continued, 'and Crane will get a nice big gold star on his very next report card.'

But it wouldn't be Crane's face in the papers, Beresford thought. Not that that really mattered. The only thing that *did* matter was arresting the bastard who'd attacked Monika, and as long as he was confident that DCI Dixon was the man for the job, he really had nothing to worry about.

The problem was, he had been growing less and less confident by the minute that DCI Dixon really *was* the man for the job.

PC Harry Nettlebury had joined the police force because he craved excitement, but it hadn't taken him long to realize that he'd have found more thrills and spills as a bouncer at the Women's Institute.

Take this latest job as a prime bloody example. There was a murderer on the loose – a man who, moreover, had left a senior police officer in a serious condition. And what part had PC Nettlebury to play in the chase? He and his partner had been driven to the woods in a police van along with half a dozen other young constables, and told to search a specific section of it inch by balls-aching inch.

That was what they been doing for the past several hours.

And what was it they were looking for?

Ah, well, you see, nobody seemed to know that, but they were not, presumably, looking for the half a dozen used contraceptives that he'd discovered during the course of his search, and, as per instructions, had bagged up.

As he searched, there was a part of him that said he had had enough of this lark, and he'd find some other line of work, but there was another part (a much more powerful part) which accepted that, while his mother had never wanted him to join the police force, she'd wring his bloody neck if he left it now.

'I think I've found something,' said PC Cowgill, Nettlebury's current partner, who was working along the other side of their allotted strip.

'More rubber johnnies?' Nettlebury asked in disgust.

'No, I think it's a woven basket of some kind,' Cowgill said.

Suddenly, the whole thing was becoming interesting.

Nettlebury turned, so that he was crouching next to his partner, and looked at Cowgill's discovery.

It certainly looked like the corner of a wicker basket, poking out of the ground from beneath a bush.

'Maybe we'd better call the skipper,' Cowgill suggested.

Bollocks! Nettlebury thought. They hadn't called the skipper when they'd found the rubber johnnies, and he could see no reason to call him now.

'I think it's wedged in some kind of hole – maybe a collapsed rabbit warren,' Cowgill said.

It seemed likely, Nettlebury thought.

'I'm going to try and prise it free,' he told his partner.

'I still think we should get the skipper,' Cowgill said worriedly.

But Nettlebury had already got a grip on the projecting corner, and was trying to coax it out of the ground.

'It's not easy,' he told his partner.

And then, suddenly it was. The basket flew out of the ground as if it had a will of its own, and Nettlebury, caught off-guard, lost his grip of it in the middle of performing an involuntary backward somersault.

By the time he righted himself, Cowgill had placed the basket on more level ground and was in the process of lifting the lid.

'Careful,' Nettlebury warned him, 'it might be a bomb!'

'Do you really think so?' Cowgill asked, pulling his hand away from the basket as if it had just burned him.

'Do I think it might be a bomb? No, not really,' Nettlebury said, lifting the lid himself.

It did not take him long to regret wresting the honour from his partner. The sandwiches, inside the basket, were being earnestly worked on by the most revolting looking maggots he had ever seen, and the stench was overpowering.

Nettlebury banged the lid down again. He gagged, but did not vomit, and after a couple of breaths of fresh air, he began to feel slightly better.

'Now you can call the skipper,' he said in a voice which, even to him, seemed half-strangled.

The two cars had been parked on Birch Avenue – one up from number 27, one down from number 27 – for nearly half an hour. Each car contained two men, and they had been carrying out what in the fashionable jargon *du jour* was called a 'target assessment survey'. What that meant in practice was they were doing their best to ensure that the men who would be carrying out phase two of the operation did not come up against any unpleasant surprises.

The men about to enact phase two were sitting in an unmarked van just up the road, dressed in full riot gear.

They had already been briefed by DCI Dixon.

'This Jim Coles is a dangerous man,' Dixon had said. 'He's killed a girl, and put a senior police officer in a coma, so I don't want you taking any unnecessary chances. On the other hand, I don't want you using unnecessary force, either, because if his brief manages to get him off on the grounds of police brutality, I'll show the officers involved what real brutality really is.'

Now, Dixon was sitting in his Mercedes-Benz, next to the unmarked van. Beside him, in the passenger seat, was DS Higgins, who was already wearing a stab-proof vest, and, once he was back inside the van, would be donning one of the heavy helmets.

They watched, as another van, this one bearing the logo of the local television network, drove slowly down the street, and came to a halt opposite number 27.

'I wasn't expecting that,' Dixon said.

'I don't imagine you were,' Higgins said, with a grin.

'So who tipped the buggers off?'

'It was probably some subordinate of yours who thought it

might be good for your image if there was film of the team that
you lead arresting a vicious murderer,' Higgins speculated.

'Yes, that was probably it,' Dixon agreed. 'What I should be
doing now is telling someone on my team to make sure that the
television van is clear of the area before I send any men in.'

'Should you, sir?' Higgins asked.

'On the other hand, the very act of moving the van on might
alert our suspect to the fact we're here, and thus make taking him
into custody a much more dangerous procedure,' Dixon mused.

'Just what I was thinking, sir,' Higgins said.

Dixon glanced down the road.

'The television people should have had time to set up by now,
so let's do it,' he said.

It was the first time any of the officers in the back of the police van
would have had to face a murderer, and the atmosphere was tense
– a mixture of subdued excitement and barely concealed fear.

'Don't worry lads, you'll do what you need to do,' Higgins told
them. 'And just think how chuffed your mums will be when they
see you on the telly.'

'How's she going to recognize me with this bloody big helmet
on?' one of the constables asked – and all the others laughed.

That was better, Higgins thought – that was the frame of mind
he wanted them in.

'Let's go,' he said to the driver.

The van moved slowly down the street, as if the driver had a
delivery to make, and was not sure he had the right address.

When it stopped in front of the suspect's house, Higgins clicked
on his radio.

'Are you in place, Team B?' he asked.

'Affirmative, we are in place,' a slightly metallic voice replied.

'Then go!' Higgins said.

The back doors of the van flew open – just as, on the street
parallel to this one, the back doors of a similar van would be flying
open – and six pairs of heavy boots hit the ground.

Now was the time when every second mattered – the time when
niceties went by the board – and with that in mind, the leading
officer did not waste time lifting the gate latch, but instead kicked
it open with his boot.

The officers rushed up the path, trampling the borders of delphiniums as they went. It took them no more than five seconds to reach the front door, and it was only another five before the bobby with the hand-held battering ram had reduced the lock to a piece of twisted junkyard metal, and had pushed open the creaking, splintered front door itself.

Higgins checked quickly over his shoulder, and saw that the news crew had – just as he'd asked them – waited until the unit had reached the front door before starting to get out of the van. By the time he emerged with the prisoner, he thought, they would be in just the right position to do the scene justice.

Then he wiped all thoughts of the media out of his mind, and stepped into the hallway.

Two of the team were already disappearing up the staircase, another two were heading down the corridor towards the kitchen, and a fifth was waiting outside the front parlour door for Higgins' instructions.

From inside the parlour, he could hear the sound of the television, but whoever was in there wasn't watching it. Whoever was in there was waiting – maybe with a knife in his hand – for someone to come through the door.

As Higgins reached out for the door handle, his heart had moved into over-drive.

It should be all right, he told himself. He was wearing both a stab-proof jacket and helmet, for God's sake. But as DCI Dixon had warned them earlier, Jim Coles had killed Mary Green and put Monika Paniatowski in hospital – and he had nothing to lose by causing another serious injury.

Higgins opened the door. Two people – a man and a woman in their late fifties – were sitting on the sofa. The woman had a china teacup in her hand, and was holding it rigidly as though she were a wax dummy. The man sat open-mouthed, his eyes fixed blankly on the flickering television screen.

They were both, understandably, in a state of shock, and had been since they had been presented with a series of noises which they had been unable to process into a coherent narrative, because nothing remotely like this had ever happened to them before.

Shocked, they might be, but Jim Coles, murderer, they certainly weren't.

Higgins held out his warrant card, confident that it was a complete waste of time.

'I'm Detective Sergeant Higgins,' he said. 'I want you to keep calm, because there's absolutely nothing to worry about.'

From overhead came the sound of banging in the bedrooms, and the couple on the sofa instinctively, though without any real comprehension, raised their eyes to the ceiling.

'Forget that for the moment!' Higgins said. 'I need to identify you. Are you Mr and Mrs Coles?'

The woman showed absolutely no reaction at all, but the man did manage a slight nod.

'We need to talk to your son, Jim, Mr Coles,' Higgins said. 'Do you know where he is?'

Coles nodded.

'So where *is* he?' Higgins asked.

Mr Coles raised a trembling hand, and pointed at the wall directly in front of him.

'Are you saying that he's next door, at number 25?' Higgins asked.

Because if he was next door, it was just possible that he might be able to slip away in all the confusion.

'No,' Mr Cole said, in a thin, broken voice, 'he's there.'

Where? He was still pointing at the bloody wall, Higgins thought.

And then he had the sickening realization that Mr Coles wasn't pointing at the wall at all, but at the fireplace, and, more specifically, at the china urn which was resting on the mantelpiece.

He walked over to the mantelpiece, to get a closer look. The urn was mounted on a small wooden plinth, and there was a brass plaque attached to the plinth.

**Jim Coles
1958-1977
A beloved son
Sadly missed**

Higgins turned, and looked out of the window. The news camera-man was in place at the shattered front gate, and the television reporter was standing beside him. He had promised them a scoop, but all he had to offer them was a fiasco.

The boss would have his balls for this, he thought – and, inside him, it felt as if someone he was very close to had just died.

Louisa sat next to her mother's bed, looking for some sign of life – for a little of the spark that she had come to associate with this woman.

There was nothing.

She took a deep breath.

'I went to school today, Mum,' she said. 'I thought it might help to follow my usual routine.' She laughed. 'I know you often think I'm not spontaneous enough, and sometimes I even agree with you – I'm half-Spanish, so just where *is* my fiery Spanish temperament? – but we are what we are, and what I am is a very orderly person. I find routine soothing. I can't help it.' She paused. 'And it's a good job one of us *is* orderly, isn't it, Mum, or goodness knows what kind of a mess we'd have found ourselves in by now.'

She stood up, and walked over to the window. The hospital was built on a rise, and from there, she could see quite a lot of the town. It wasn't much of a place, she thought, really not much of a place at all.

People were always complaining that there was nothing to do and nothing to see. And she agreed with them, in many ways. Yet when she'd been offered the possibility of escape – been offered not just a place at Cambridge, but a *scholarship* – she'd turned it down, partly because she really did want to be a police officer, but partly because she didn't want to leave Whitebridge behind.

She went back to the bed.

'I did playground duty, Mum,' she said. 'Well, it was my turn. And I saw something really interesting. There was this group of girls of very different ages in this really serious conversation, and I know for a fact that one of them – you don't know her – virtually never speaks to anybody. In fact, she reminds me a lot of Mary Green. Mary doesn't – didn't – ever really want to join in with things. She didn't work very hard, either. I'm sure she was at least as bright as John, but while he's always been near the top of the class, she's seemed happy just to coast along. And that's strange, isn't it, considering how close they are?'

A moan – as deep and miserable as any moan was ever likely to be – drifted down the corridor and through the door.

Louisa shivered, and though the room was not cold, she turned up the collar of her blazer.

'And then the strangest thing happened, Mum,' she continued. 'John Green went over to the girls, and suddenly all their worries seemed to just melt away. Do you think that's because he's so good looking that they just go gooey at the sight of him? Or do you think it's something else? Does he have the power to inspire calm? Because some people do, you know.'

There'd been absolutely no change in her mother since she'd entered the room, she thought. She'd talked about her day, and tried to make it interesting, but she might just as well have talked mumbo-jumbo.

She might just as well not have been there at all!

That's not true, she told herself. Even if Mum can't hear me – or can hear me, but can't make any sense of the words – I'm sure it helps her that I'm here.

'I want you to get better, Mum,' she said, feeling her lower lip tremble as she spoke. 'I want you to get better – because if you don't, I just don't know how I'm going to handle everything.'

EIGHT

They had all already decided, independently, that it would be an act of cowardice not to return to the Drum and Monkey, so when Beresford had suggested it, the other two had immediately agreed.

Now they were sitting at that usual table, pints of ale in front of Beresford and Crane, a bitter lemon in front of Meadows – and a gap where there should have been a neat vodka.

'Rhino has done no canvassing of the neighbours, and he hasn't talked to anybody at the school that Mary attended,' Beresford complained. 'Instead, he fixated on this motorcyclist, and has gone charging after him like a . . . well, like a bloody rhino.'

'To be fair, sir, it is more than likely that the motorcyclist is the murderer,' Crane pointed out.

'Yes, it is,' Beresford agreed, 'but that shouldn't mean we

abandon all other lines of investigation. And even if he is the killer, Rhino doesn't know *why* he wanted to kill her, or *why* he chose to drive her out to the stately home to kill her, when it would have been easier – and probably much safer – to kill her near her home. And why does that matter, Jack?'

'It matters because all the evidence we have so far is circumstantial, so unless something else much more concrete turns up, we're going to need a confession,' Crane said.

'Exactly,' Beresford agreed. 'Now, we all know there have been cases where the moment the feller's in custody, he breaks down and confesses. But most of the people we arrest – especially if they're amateurs, who still think they're smarter than we are – will deny everything, and it's only through patient, painstaking investigation that we get them to break down. And to conduct that kind of interrogation we need facts – which we don't bloody have.'

Jesus, he thought as he finished, that sounded just like the boss – and he didn't know whether to feel proud or depressed about it.

'There's something very wrong about everyone I've met connected to Mary Green and her family,' Kate Meadows said. 'They're all odd in their own ways, it's true, but, at the same time, there seems to be an overarching net of strangeness that unites them.'

'Are you telling us that you think they're all part of a conspiracy?' Beresford asked.

'Yes, I rather think I am,' Meadows confessed.

'And that it was this conspiracy which murdered Mary Green?'

'Good God, no!' Meadows exclaimed. 'The idea of Mr and Mrs Green and Mrs Brown being part of a murder plot is ludicrous. But the conspiracy may have been a contributory factor in her death – in other words, she might have been killed because she was *connected* to the conspiracy.'

'I'd like to hear more about these people,' Beresford said.

Meadows told him about Mary's parents, and how they seemed to defer in everything to their son, John. Then she outlined the meeting she and Higgins had had with Mrs Brown.

'An old woman, with chronic arthritis, decides to move away from her home to a place where she has no friends,' she summed up at the end. 'That, you have to admit, is insane. But as chance will have it, she lands on her feet – or on her swollen ankles, anyway. A girl – whose name she can no longer remember – volunteers, through some unspecified process – to look after her at the weekends. And when this girl can no longer do the job, Mary Green – a sixth former who has both her work to do and her life to live – agrees to spend every weekend with her. How's that for improbable?'

'And you think this Roger Smith feller is part of it, too?' Beresford asked.

'Yes, because not only does he seem to have spent quite a lot of time with John, Mary's brother, but he was so keen to deny he knew Mrs Brown that he didn't even bother to establish which Mrs Brown I was talking about.'

'The first thing in the morning, we start doing the sort of canvassing that Rhino should have done already,' Beresford said. He grinned, wryly. 'It would be good if we could leave most of the donkey work to the rest of the team, but there is no rest of the team.'

'We'll manage, sir,' Crane said. 'How could we not, when we're all such smart cookies.'

'You're right,' Beresford agreed. He sighed. 'I wish Monika was here.'

He was not even aware he'd said those last five words aloud, until he noticed that the other two were nodding.

'I could have had anyone I wanted,' Doris Dixon used to say in the early days of their marriage.

And he'd believed her, because she'd been a pretty thing – maybe even beautiful – and he'd noticed the way that men turned their heads towards her when she walked into a room.

'Yes, I could have anyone, William,' she'd say, 'but I like big men, and you were the biggest I knew, so I chose you.'

At first, he'd sometimes still found it hard to believe that a woman like her could select someone like him (even if he was the biggest man she knew!).

He'd considered himself very lucky, indeed, for well over a year – and then the honeymoon feeling started wearing a bit thin.

He no longer considered himself lucky. He no longer believed she could have had any man she wanted. Other men, he now thought – men who were better looking than him, and knew that they had more than one shot at winning a good-looking girl – had seen beyond and below the surface. They had recognized the vinegary harridan who lurked within Doris, and had shied away – leaving the ground clear for him to fall right into the trap.

He could have divorced her, but he was a strict Catholic and did not believe in divorce.

He could have murdered her, but he had been in the job long enough to know that it was almost impossible to get away with a domestic murder.

He sometimes prayed – though he knew he shouldn't – that she would catch some lethal, but mercifully painless, disease, and he would be shut of her. But in the meantime, there was nothing to do but endure her – deflecting the barbs as best he could, and just getting on with life.

As he arrived at his home, an hour after the raid, he was hoping that Doris had gone out with some of her friends, but then he saw her waiting for him on the doorstep.

'You've been on television,' she said.

That was the reason she was standing where she was – because she couldn't wait to rub it in – he thought.

'Yes, I know I've been on television,' he said wearily, brushing past her and heading for the living room, where the cocktail cabinet was located.

'Tell me about it,' she said, following him.

He took a bottle of whisky out of the cabinet, and poured himself a generous measure.

'You don't want to hear about it,' he said.

'But I do,' she insisted. 'I want all the details.'

He sighed. 'There was a motorcycle caught on CCTV that we suspected was being ridden by the killer. We ran down the license plate, and found it belonged to a Jim Coles. We went round to his house—'

'Quite *a lot* of you went round to his house,' Doris interrupted.

'That was no more than a sensible precaution. If he was our killer, there was a good chance he'd turn out to be violent.'

'But he wasn't, was he – because he was dead.'

'Yes, he was dead.'

'He'd *been* dead for more than six months, it said on the news.

He crashed his motorbike – the one you thought you saw on camera – into a big wagon. The bike was a complete write-off. So maybe it was a *ghost bike* you saw on the tape.'

'It wasn't a ghost bike,' Dixon said, taking a deep swig of his whisky. 'It was a different bike, using Jim Coles' plates.'

'Well, you have got egg on your face, haven't you?' Doris asked. 'I can't see any of the other men I might have married getting themselves into such a pickle.'

He really hated her at that moment, he thought – but not as much as he hated DS Higgins and DI Marsden.

Elena was out for the night, and Louisa had just put the twins to bed when she heard the knock on the front door. She expected the caller to be either Kate Meadows (who'd said she'd call in later) or one of the neighbours, so it was something of a surprise, when she opened the door, to find John Green standing there.

For a moment, he just looked at her blankly and helplessly, as if he'd had his script all worked out mentally, but it had somehow slipped out of his head during his walk up the garden path.

Finally, he did speak.

'Hi,' he said.

'Hi,' Louisa replied.

'I just called to find out . . . you know . . . how your mother is getting on,' John said awkwardly.

'There's been no change,' Louisa said.

'That's a pity,' John said, 'although it's a lot better than if there was a change, and it was, you know, a change in the wrong direction.' He shrugged, helplessly. 'I shouldn't have put it like that. In fact, I really shouldn't have come here at all, should I?'

He had been rather gauche, she thought, but at least he seemed to mean well. They had never really had much to do with each other in school, even though they were both members of the Upper Sixth, but at that moment, she felt a real sense of warmth for him.

'Why don't you come inside for a coffee?' she suggested.

He shrugged. 'I don't want to be any trouble.'

'You'll be no trouble at all,' she told him. 'I was going to make one for myself anyway.'

They had their coffee at the breakfast bar in the kitchen. For a while, they chatted about the inter-house competition (they were in rival houses, and the battle to win the school house of the year trophy was currently on a knife edge between them), but neither of them could raise much enthusiasm for the subject at that moment, and Louisa began to regret ever asking him in.

Finally, just as she was about to remark that she'd probably kept him there far longer than he'd been intending to stay, John said, 'Listen, Louisa, I wasn't being strictly truthful earlier.'

'Oh?' she said, noncommittally, wondering why else he could possibly have called. 'Is that right?'

'Yes, it is,' he said. 'When I said I'd come here to ask about your mother's health, I was lying. Or rather, I was and I wasn't. I want your mother to get better – we all do – but that wasn't why I came.'

'Why did you come?' Louisa said.

'I want to ask you a favour.'

A favour! How could she do a favour for *him*?

'I'm listening,' she said.

'They're cremating my sister tomorrow,' John said. He forced back a sob. 'I loved her very much.'

'I'm sure you did,' Louisa said.

'The funeral would have been much easier to bear if I'd had her by my side.' John laughed bitterly. 'But, of course, if I'd had her by my side, there wouldn't be any need for a funeral.'

'You wanted me to do you a favour,' Louisa reminded him gently.

'My mum and dad can't face going, but I want somebody by my side for support, and since we've both lost . . . sorry, I didn't mean that, you still haven't lost your mother yet, of course . . . What I meant was, you're in a better position than anyone to know how I'm feeling, and I'd really appreciate it if you could be there for me.'

It wasn't an easy request to turn down, Louisa thought, but maybe, since she really didn't want to do it, she could find a way to get him to withdraw the offer.

'Look,' she said, 'we're in the same year in school, and we've chatted now and again, but I'm not sure I'm the right person for this.'

'You don't want to do it,' John said. He stood up. 'That's quite understandable, Louisa, I can see that now, and I should never have asked.'

'It's not so much that I don't want to do it as that there must be lots of people who would be more appropriate,' Louisa protested.

'There aren't,' John said firmly. 'We're a very close family, and we don't really know anybody else on a personal level.'

'There were those four girls in the playground, earlier in the day . . .' Louisa began.

'Which girls?' he demanded. 'Who are you talking about?'

His sudden vehemence took her by surprise. 'You know the ones,' she said. 'Jennifer Black was one, and there were three other younger ones whose names I don't know.'

'You saw me talking to them,' he said.

'Yes, I did.'

He relaxed a little. 'They were just upset about Mary,' he said. 'Perhaps she'd been kind to them at some time, because although she didn't make a great song and dance about it, she was a kind girl at heart.'

'I'm sure she was,' Louisa said.

'But I didn't really know them myself,' John continued. He looked straight into her eyes. 'And I hardly know you, either – but at least we both know what it's like to suffer.'

'All right,' Louisa said, 'I'll do it. But if you change your mind, I won't be in the least offended.'

'I won't change my mind,' John said, and then he leant forward and kissed her lightly on the cheek. He jumped back, as if his lips had been scalded. 'There I go making a mess of things again,' he said bitterly.

'No, it's all right, I'm not offended,' Louisa told him.

'I'd better go before I do anything else foolish,' John said. 'It's really very kind of you, and if you ever need me to do something . . .' He shook his head. 'I really had better go. I can find my own way out.'

In his youth, Stan Kershaw had been able to knock back six or seven pints before going to bed, and still sleep through the night. Those days were long gone. *These* days, if he had more than a couple of gills at the Crown and Anchor, he could pretty much guarantee he'd have to get up two or three times in the night.

He didn't mind these nocturnal journeys, because he always fell asleep again as soon as he was back in bed. Besides, he rather liked being up at a time when everyone else was out for the count.

It was peaceful.

It was quiet.

And when he looked out of his bathroom window down onto Dardanelles Road, he could picture – without any aspects of modern life getting in the way – the old days, when horse-drawn carts from the countryside trundled down it on their way to Whitebridge market.

He was out of luck that night, as far as peace and quiet to pursue his memories went, he told himself, as he watched a black van make its way along the street, and come to a halt at number seventeen.

It must be two o'clock in the morning, he thought. That was a bloody funny time to be calling on anybody.

No sooner had the van stopped, than the front door opened, and two people emerged carrying suitcases.

That would be Mr and Mrs Jones, Stan thought, and realized that though they'd lived opposite him for five years, he still didn't know their first names. He didn't know what Mr Jones did for a living, either. Occasionally, he'd notice him leaving the house with a leather briefcase, but that could mean he was anything from a bookie's runner to a bank manager.

Mrs Jones climbed into the van, and Mr Jones went back to lock the front door.

It wasn't like the old days, Stan thought. When people who fell behind with their rent did a moonlight flit back then, they'd take their furniture with them – aye, and sometimes even furniture that wasn't theirs at all.

He wondered, briefly, where they were going, and why they were leaving at that time of night. They could be going on their holidays, he supposed – he'd read that, these days, aeroplanes took off at some bloody funny times.

He finished his pee, carefully replaced his withered organ back in his pyjamas, and shuffled back to his bedroom.

By the time he was climbing into his bed, he'd forgotten all about the Jones family.

*   *   *

Mrs Brown suddenly became aware that there was someone there in the bedroom with her.

'I can hear you breathing,' she said. 'Who is it?'

'It's only me,' said a familiar, reassuring voice. 'I'd like you to put on your bedside light.'

'Why have you come, Trus—?'

'Shush, don't call me that,' he interrupted her. 'Call me Mr Smith.'

'Even here? Even now?'

'We can never be too careful.'

'Of course not. Why are you here, Mr Smith?'

'I have come to tell you that we are leaving,' he said.

'I thought that might be it,' she replied. 'Is it my fault?' she asked, with a tremble in her voice.

'Yes, it is your fault,' he said. 'The girl was put into your care, and you did not take the care of her that you should have taken.'

'I'm sorry,' Mrs Brown said. 'But when you saw how happy it made her when I—'

'We are not put on this earth to be happy,' Mr Smith said, perhaps a little harshly.

'No, no, of course not,' Mrs Brown agreed.

'I want you to know that what I have to say next is in no way a punishment for your sins,' Mr Smith said. 'How could it be, when they are already completely forgiven?'

'Thank you.'

'No, what I am about to say is much more practical – more concerned with matters of survival.' He paused. 'We are going, but *this* time, we cannot take you with us.'

'I understand,' she said. 'I am too old. I would only slow you down, and that would be fatal.'

Mr Smith smiled. 'It would indeed. We cannot let the fate of the universe be dependent on the thin shoulders of one old woman.'

'I know that,' she said.

'Then do you also know this?' he asked. 'We cannot take you with us – but we cannot leave you behind, either.'

'Yes, I know that too,' she said.

He walked over to her bedside, and placed a small brown bottle on the table. 'I supervised the making of this myself,' he said.

'You must wait for an hour, and then you must take it.' He paused. 'You won't fail me, will you?'

'No, I won't fail you,' she promised. 'Will it hurt?'

'When compared to the suffering you have endured from your arthritic joints, it will be as nothing,' he promised. 'And it will be quick.'

'Will God blame me for taking my own life?' she asked.

'No,' he said, 'God will know – as we all know – that you only did it for His greater glory.' He glanced down at his watch. 'I must leave you now.'

'But we will meet again in glory?'

'Yes, if we are successful in our quest, we will certainly meet again in glory,' he said.

And then he was gone.

NINE

Tuesday

Given all the coverage on the television, and the front page headlines in the morning papers, there wasn't anyone in the CID suite – not even those who had nothing to do with the investigation – who didn't feel a sense of dread about the imminent arrival of DCI Dixon.

When he did finally arrive, the walls did not actually shake, nor did the overhead lights flicker – but it certainly felt as if they did.

'Last night, I took part in a raid on a house in Birch Avenue,' he told his team – and anyone else within fifty yards. 'The reason I authorized that raid was because DI Marsden and DS Higgins had assured me that we'd find Mary Green's killer there.' His angry eyes swept the room. 'Where is DI Marsden?' he demanded.

For a moment, no one spoke, then DS Higgins sighed and said, 'He's with the telephone team in the incident room, sir. We've made an appeal for information regarding the motorbike and we're expecting—'

'Now that really is convenient for DI Marsden, isn't it?' Dixon

said. 'Talk about a gutless wonder. But he can't hide away forever.'
He paused. 'Now where was I?'

There was another silence, then Beresford said, 'You were talking about the raid, sir.'

'Ah yes, the raid! We didn't catch Jim Coles, did we, DS Higgins?'

'No, sir,' Higgins mumbled.

'I can't hear you, sergeant,' Dixon said. 'Speak up!'

Higgins raised his head. 'No, sir, we didn't,' he said.

'And why was that?'

'Because he was dead.'

'Because he was dead! And don't you think, sergeant, that you should have checked up on that before we went into his parents' house mob handed?'

'I'm sorry, sir,' Higgins said.

'Oh, there's no need to apologize,' Dixon told him. 'I love being made to look a bloody idiot in the papers and on television. It's a lifetime ambition which – thanks to you – I've finally achieved.' He paused to light a cigarette. 'I suppose you'd better brief us on developments since that monumental cock-up, sergeant – if, indeed, there have *been* any developments.'

Yesterday, I was the golden boy, Higgins thought miserably – and now, as far as the boss is concerned, I'm less than dog shit.

He was going to have to climb back into Dixon's favour very quickly, he told himself, because if he didn't, the rest of the team (who had always resented his favoured status) would attack him like the wounded animal he was and rip him to shreds.

'Jim Coles' bike was a write-off,' he said, 'so what we saw going through the West Gate on the CCTV film was almost certainly a stolen bike, which was using Jim Coles' registration plates. So what we've done is to appeal to all riders of Honda 250cc bikes to come and register with us. We've also appealed to any members of the public to ring the hotline if they notice that somebody who *used* to ride a Honda 250cc suddenly isn't riding it anymore.'

It would have been nice to get a grunt of approval at that point, but Dixon said nothing.

'We're also approaching it from the other angle,' Higgins ploughed on, 'which is to trace the route of the licence plate from the dead boy's motorbike to the one in the closed circuit television pictures.'

Dixon snorted. 'Anything else?'

Higgins shifted uncomfortably. 'We've examined the picnic basket for prints,' he said. 'There are three sets on the metal parts, though one set has been virtually obliterated by one of the others. Of the two good sets we have, one belongs to the dead girl and the other set is unknown to us, which means that our prime suspect has either been a very *good* boy up to now or a very *lucky* one.' He hesitated, wondering whether or not he dared to inject a positive note into the briefing, then said, 'If it's the latter – if he's just been lucky – I think we can say that now we're on his trail, his luck is about to run out.'

'Maybe,' Dixon said, 'but of course, when the people chasing you are the Keystone Kops, your luck can sometimes hold out for ever.' He turned his attention to Beresford. 'And what about you, Colin?' he asked, his voice suddenly much milder and friendlier. 'What have you got planned for your little team?'

'If it's all right with you, sir, we'd like to find out more about Mary Green's family and their associates,' Beresford said.

'Excellent idea,' Dixon told him. 'Juries love background material, because it tells them a story, and while the background might not have that much to do with the case that's being presented, it does help persuade the twelve good men – or do I say persons, now?'

'I believe it's correct to say persons, sir,' Beresford told him.

'It does help persuade twelve good persons that we actually know what we're doing – and that can only strengthen the prosecution's case. Do you agree with that, Colin?'

'Yes, sir, I do,' Beresford said.

But what he was thinking was – I've just been given permission to choose any toys I like, as long as I take them into some quiet corner, and play with them by myself.

Winifred Goodman was built (to use a phrase that was still popular in the all-male bars of the working men's clubs) like a brick shithouse. Her arms were thick, her thighs were sturdy, her hips were designed to balance sacks of sugar on, and her backside could fill a telephone box all on its own.

Winifred had always been of an optimistic nature. When she'd been a little girl, back in Jamaica, she dreamed of becoming a doctor, and though she'd never achieved that ambition – had instead, attained the much less exalted position of home help – she felt all right about that, too. She liked looking after people, and she was very good at it. And why would God have given her such a fine strong pair of arms, if not so that she could turn over mattresses and help her old people in and out of the bath?

When she got to Sebastopol Street that morning, the first thing she did was reach in her bag for her bunch of keys (she had so many of them that she sometimes felt like one of the housekeepers in the old black and white English films that she'd watched in the open-air cinemas back home), and select the right one for Mrs Brown's door.

She opened the door, and stepped over the threshold into the hallway.

'I'm coming in, Mrs Brown,' she said. 'You just got time to hide your boyfriend under the bed.'

She laughed at her own joke. One of her clients had got offended at a similar remark, and reported her to her supervisor, who'd called her into his office.

'You just can't go saying things like that to clients, Mrs Goodman,' he'd said sternly.

'Just my bit o' fun,' she'd replied, looking down at the desk. 'Some of de old ladies and gentlemen like it.'

'And some of them *don't*,' her supervisor had retorted. 'So in future, I'd like you to think before you speak.'

'Yes, sir, I will,' she'd said.

And she'd meant it, because she wouldn't tell a deliberate lie to anybody, and especially not to her supervisor. But somehow it hadn't made any difference – whether she wanted them to or not, the words still kept coming out of her mouth.

She stepped into the parlour/bedroom, and looked down at Mrs Brown, who appeared to be quite dead to the world.

'Well, aren't you a lazybones today?' Winifred said. 'You're going to have to wake up, you know, because I'm only here for half an hour, and we've got a lot to do in that time.'

But her words seemed to have no effect. In fact, Mrs Brown seemed to be more unconscious than asleep.

And then Winifred noticed the small brown bottle on the bedside cabinet, and the cork which was lying beside it.

She picked up the bottle and took a sniff. She didn't know what it was, but it certainly wasn't very nice.

'Lordy, Lordy,' she said.

She couldn't remember the last time she'd used that particular phrase.

When Mrs Hodges put the fried breakfast in front of her son, Barry, he looked first at his plate, then at his mother, and said, 'Do you actually want me to eat that? Look at it! It's disgusting!'

'It was all right fifteen minutes ago, Barry, when I first called you,' his mother said.

'Well, if you think I'm going to eat it now, you want your head examining,' her son said.

Mrs Hodges picked up the plate, took it over to the sink, and scraped the contents into the bin.

'It seems such a shame to waste good food,' she said. She paused, waiting for him to apologize, but she had low expectations of his ever doing that, and after a few moments had passed, she said, 'Would you like me to cook you another fry up?'

'No time,' Barry said, pouring himself a large bowl of Kellogg's Rice Krispies.

'Yes, you have,' his mother replied, glancing up at the clock. 'It'll only take you ten minutes, on that bike of yours, to—'

'I'll be catching the bus,' Barry said, drenching the Krispies in cold milk.

'Is something wrong with your bike?' his mother asked.

'No, there's nothing wrong with it,' the boy told her. 'I just don't have it any more.'

'You surely haven't got rid of it, have you, Barry?' his mother asked, shocked.

'If I haven't still got it, I must have got rid of it, mustn't I?' Barry asked angrily. 'Unless, of course, it's run away to join the circus.'

'But you loved that bike,' his mother said. 'It was your pride and joy. Whatever possessed you to get rid of it?'

Not that it's any of your business, you stupid old bitch, but I got rid of it because I don't want to end up being charged with murder, Barry Hodges thought viciously.

But aloud, all he said was, 'If you must know, it was repossessed

because I couldn't keep up the payments. All right?' He was almost
shouting by this point. 'Are you happy now?'

His mother frowned. 'But *why* couldn't you keep the payments
up? You earn good money at the supermarket, and it's not as if I
charge you anything for your bed and board.'

There were times when he could strangle her, he thought – times
when he felt an almost overwhelming urge to grab his mother by
her scrawny neck and then squeeze and squeeze until he heard
that rattle which would tell him that she would never annoy anyone
again.

'I've got other expenses,' he said.

'What other expenses do you mean?' his mother wondered. And
then it came to her. 'You've been wasting all your money on that
girl, haven't you?' she said, accusingly.

How the hell did his mother know about Mary? he wondered,
as the pit of his stomach opened up, and attempted to suck his
heart into it.

'Just what girl are we talking about here?' he said, defensively.

'You know very well what girl,' his mother said. 'The one
you've been seeing every Sunday for the last two months or so.'

'Oh, you mean Joan Mills?' he asked, cunningly.

'I don't know what her name is, but I can't imagine she's up
to much if you need to keep her away from your own mother.'

He hadn't kept her away because he'd wanted to, he thought
– he'd done it because she'd insisted that was the way it had to
be. It had driven him mad at the time that he couldn't show off
such a good-looking girl to his mates, but now he was grateful
– oh so grateful – that they had kept their relationship a secret.

If you hold your nerve, you can still get away with it, he told
himself. If you hold your nerve, it might still go away.

'Oh, I know what I wanted to ask you,' his mother said. 'Do
you know what happened to the picnic basket?'

Oh shit! he thought.

'Well?' his mother asked.

'What picnic basket?' he said.

And while he was speaking, another – completely separate –
voice in his head, a voice that didn't seem to belong to him at all,
was screaming, 'Why did you leave it behind? Why did you leave
it behind?'

'I didn't even know we had a picnic basket,' he said aloud.

'Yes, you did,' his mother contradicted him. 'It's made of wick-erwork, and it has a blue and white check lining inside. When your dad was still alive, we were always having picnics. Don't you remember?'

'No.'

'You must do. Anyway, your Auntie Elsie asked if she could borrow it, and I went up to the lumber room, which is where it's supposed to be, and it's not there at all.'

His hands itched to throttle her.

'I haven't seen it,' he said. 'I promise you, I haven't seen it.'

'Well, there's only you and me that could have taken it, and I know it wasn't me.'

He stood up, and flung his cereal bowl across the room. Milk and Rice Krispies cascaded from it as it flew through the air, then it hit the tiles on the far wall and shattered.

'I told you, I've never seen the bloody basket,' Barry screamed, 'and don't you dare tell anybody that I have.'

Crane was talking to the headmaster's secretary when the head-master himself marched importantly through his outer office towards his inner sanctum.

'Excuse me, headmaster, but this police officer would like to have a few words with you,' the secretary said.

The headmaster came to a halt, almost at his door, and when he turned around, his face was wearing an expression that could only have been called busy man's irritation.

'I've got quite enough to do, what with dealing with . . .' he began. And then he noticed Crane's tie. 'I say, you're an Oxford man,' he continued, in a much friendlier tone.

'Indeed I am,' Crane agreed.

'So am I,' the headmaster said.

'Is that right?' asked Crane, who, the moment he'd seen the notice on the school gate announcing that the headmaster was Geoffrey Tideswell, MA (Oxon), had gone home to change his tie.

'Whatever it is you want, it won't take too much of my time, I hope,' the headmaster said.

'No more than a few minutes,' Crane promised.

'Then by all means step into my study,' the headmaster invited.

Once inside, Crane looked around at the dark panelled walls, rows of awards, framed certificates and sporting trophies.

'I'm most impressed,' he said.

And he was not lying, for rarely had he seen pretentiousness on such a grand scale.

'So what can I do for you?' the headmaster asked. 'Is it anything to do with the murder?'

'In a way,' Crane said. 'I'd like to talk to two of your sixth formers – Michael Gray and Philip Jones.'

'Could you be a little more specific about why you wish to talk to them?' the headmaster asked.

Specifically, it's because we're starting on the assumption that there's something weird about the Green family, and are working our way outwards, Crane thought. And part of that process is to talk to the two lads who supposedly were playing board games with John Green and Roger Smith at the time Mary Green was being murdered.

'I'm afraid that given the nature of my investigation, I can't be specific at all,' Crane said.

'Then I'm not sure that without their parents being present . . .'

'The school is *in loco parentis*, so all that the law requires is that a member of your staff be present during the questioning,' Crane said.

'Is that right?' the headmaster asked, dubiously.

'Oh yes,' Crane said. 'It's clearly stated in paragraph fifty-three, sub-section c, of the Criminal Law Code.'

Jesus, he thought, I'm getting as good at making things up as Kate Meadows is!

Or should that be as *bad* as Kate Meadows?

'Well, I suppose that would be all right,' the headmaster conceded. 'The person you should talk to now is my secretary, Elizabeth. She can tell you where the boys are, and arrange for a member of my pastoral care team to be there when you talk to them.'

It turned out that while the headmaster called the school secretary Elizabeth, everyone else knew her as Liz, and she had worked not only for this headmaster but also for the previous two ones.

'Oh yes, I've seen them come and go,' she said. 'They sweep

in here thinking they're going to revolutionize the whole of the educational process, and in the end, all they come up with is a new way of collecting the dinner money.'

Crane grinned. 'I need to see these two lads,' he said, holding out a piece of paper with the boys' names on it.

'Well, our first step is to make sure that they're actually in school today,' Liz said.

She reached under her desk and came up with a long thin red attendance register, the sight of which was enough to take Crane immediately back to his own childhood.

Liz opened the register, and ran an expert eye down the columns of diagonal strokes.

'You're out of luck with Michael Gray,' she said. 'He's not in school today. Oh, and there's a surprise, Philip Jones isn't, either. How strange it is that they're both off on the same day.'

'Maybe I'm just unlucky,' Crane said.

'It's especially strange since they've each got a perfect attendance record for the term,' Liz said, having scanned the rest of that page of the register.

Crane felt a sudden emptiness inside him.

'Do they have any brothers or sisters in the school?' he asked.

'Let me see,' Liz said, reaching into a filing cabinet and pulling out a couple of khaki-coloured envelopes. 'Yes, Michael has two sisters and Philip has a brother and sister.'

'Could you check if they're here today?' Crane asked.

More bright red registers appeared, more columns were quickly scanned by the secretary's eyes.

'No, funnily enough, they're all absent,' Liz said. 'They've probably all gone down with the same bug. We get a lot of that.'

But it wasn't illness that was keeping them away from school, Crane thought – he was sure it wasn't that.

The blonde nurse helped the porter to decant the old woman from the trolley to the bed, then turned to the doctor and said, 'What are her chances?'

'Rather good,' said the doctor, who was there less to impart information than to seize his opportunity to flirt with the nurse. 'When she wakes up, she'll feel rather sore inside, but then a stomach pump will do that to you, and on the whole, I'd say she's got off rather lightly.'

The nurse picked up the board which had been clipped onto the edge of the bed.

'Religion unknown,' she read. 'I thought all old women were confirmed churchgoers – if not for the company and warmth, then at least for the heavenly insurance.'

'You're a very cynical young woman,' the doctor said, 'which makes you just the sort of person we very much need in the modern nursing profession. And maybe you're right about most of them, but according to her home help – who we call Hallelujah Winifred, because if you get too close to her when she's singing one of her hymns, she can burst your ear drum – Mrs Brown has never shown the least tendency towards, or interest in, religion.'

'She has no friends or relatives, either,' the nurse said, consulting the board again.

'Again, that can happen to anyone if they just happen to live long enough,' the doctor said.

'Do you know, it almost seems as if she wasn't a real person at all,' the nurse said.

If she hadn't been such an attractive blonde, the doctor would have told her not to be so fanciful.

But she *was* an attractive blonde – one, moreover, who he had hopes of eventually mounting, and so he said indulgently, 'And what, pray, leads you to that conclusion?'

The nurse shrugged. 'No religion, no family and perhaps the most boring surname in the English language,' she said. 'It's like someone with a very limited imagination had made her up.'

'So she has a common name,' the doctor said. 'Lots of people do. That's what makes it common.'

Frank Brough wasn't happy about having a detective visit his motorcycle shop, especially when the detective in question was the dogged DS Higgins.

'It's such a long time since our paths have crossed, Frank,' Higgins said jovially, looking around the shop. 'I think I was still on the beat the last time we had a run-in.'

'Well, you see, there's no reason for our paths to cross, Mr Higgins, because you're a policeman and I'm an honest businessman.'

'Is that what you are?' Higgins asked sceptically.

'It is – and if you look around the shop, you'll see that I'm doing all right for myself.'

'So no more chopping up bikes for spare parts for you, then, Frank?' Higgins asked.

'I never—'

'No more stuffing nicked bikes into packing cases and shipping them across the water to the Republic of Ireland.'

'Now you were never able to prove I was involved in any of that, Mr Higgins,' Brough said.

'No, I wasn't,' Higgins agreed. 'But we both know it went on, don't we?' He grinned. 'Still, that's all water under the bridge now, and what concerns me today is Jim Coles.'

'Jim Coles? Jim Coles,' Brough repeated, as if the name was totally unfamiliar to him.

'Jim was a young motorcyclist who learned at great personal cost that you can't argue with a lorry,' Higgins said.

'That's right. Jim Coles! I know who he was now. He rode a Honda 250, didn't he?'

'And after the crash, the bike was delivered to your shop, wasn't it? Now why was that?'

'I do the assessments for the insurers. You see, it's not worth them sending one of their head office fellers down here, so I act as their agent.'

'It's a very responsible job,' Higgins said. 'They must trust you.'

'Like I said, I'm a respectable businessman.'

'So what did you say about the bike in your report to the insurance company, Frank?'

'I said the bike was a complete write-off – which it was.'

'And what happened to it after that?'

'I sent it down to the scrap yard for crushing.'

'Well, there you are, all my questions are answered,' Higgins said. 'Thank you for your time, sir.' He walked towards the door, then stopped and turned around. 'No, I was wrong – there is one more question I still need to ask. What happened to the plates?'

'The plates?'

'The licence plates, which, strictly speaking, are government property and should be returned to the appropriate authority once they cease to be used on a vehicle.'

'The plates were as much a write-off as the rest of the bike,' Brough said. 'You won't believe this – I wouldn't have believed it myself, if I hadn't seen it with my own eyes – but they'd sort of melded into the general bodywork.'

'You're right there, Frank – I don't believe it,' Higgins said. 'But maybe I will when you've shown me the photographs.'

'What photographs?'

Higgins laughed. 'The insurance company may not have felt it was worth sending one of its people here, but they'll have wanted more proof than just your say-so. What they'll have wanted, I should imagine, is photographs of the bike from every angle. I'm right, aren't I?'

'You're right,' Brough agreed, sounding more and more concerned with every second that passed, 'but I don't have them anymore.'

'No problem,' Higgins said cheerfully. 'I expect the insurance company will have them on file.'

Brough licked his lips, which suddenly felt incredibly dry.

'Mr Higgins . . .' he began.

'Here's the thing,' Higgins said. 'We both know you took the plates off that bike and sold them on, but if I take you in, you'll come up with some cock and bull story about how the shop was burgled one night and the plates were stolen, but it didn't seem worth reporting because . . .'

'Mr Higgins . . .' Brough said again.

'I haven't finished, sunshine,' Higgins said harshly, 'and if you've got any sense, you'll shut up, because what I'm about to tell you is to your advantage. I could do all that, but it would take time, and while I might eventually be able to charge you as an accessory before the fact in a murder—'

'What!'

'. . . an accessory before the fact in a murder, I've got bigger fish to fry than you. So all I want from you, my son, is the name of the man you sold the plates to, and then I'll be on my way. Do you get what I'm saying?'

'I get it,' Brough said miserably.

Monika Paniatowski is back in the woods, and this time it is so real that she can smell the fresh leaves and feel the spongy soil beneath her feet.

And there is much less confusion, too, this time.

She knows she's not in the woods to see her father, because he is a long time dead.

She knows she's not in the woods as part of an investigation into the murder of a journalist, because that case has been closed for two years, and the poor soul responsible for the murder is behind bars.

And she knows she is not about to be raped, because that rape is in the past, too, and only the consequences are there to greet her every morning with their smiles and complaints.

But this visit does have something to do with the rape, because she is doing what she now tells herself she should have done a long time ago – returning to the scene of her nightmare, in an attempt to bury her fears.

It is not easy, but she never thought it would be.

Every step she takes, it gets harder, and there is at least a part of her which feels that she has already been brave enough, and now is the time for a tactical retreat, followed by a large, neat vodka.

But she will not back down. She will carry on until she reaches the very spot at which she was violated, and she will stand there, looking down at it, and telling herself that it is all over – that it has nothing to do with the life she is living now, and can have nothing to do with that life.

It is because she is so wrapped up in facing the past that the actual person she passes – going in the opposite direction, and carrying a picnic basket – seems less real to her than the ghostly spectres she is on her way to defeat. She notices him, of course, and later – when it is all over – she will probably wonder what he was doing in the woods. But for now, he barely registers in her emotion-wracked mind.

The ground rises slightly for a while, then gently falls away, creating a little dip, and when she is just on the edge of the dip, she sees the girl.

There can be no doubt that she's dead – none at all.

Monika reaches into her handbag, wondering if she has coverage on her police radio.

And that is the last thing she remembers.

TEN

A seasoned, battle-scarred doctor would barely have given Meadows's warrant card a glance, but this one was young and still idealistic enough to want to do everything by the book.

'So how can I help you, detective sergeant?' he asked, when he'd examined the warrant card from all possible angles.

'I'd like you to tell me about Mrs Brown,' Meadows said.

'But why would you want to know about her?' the doctor asked, suspiciously. 'Attempted suicide is not a criminal offence in this country – it hasn't been for a number of years.'

'We think this particular suicide attempt may be tied in with a murder we're investigating.'

'Ah!' the doctor said.

'So what *can* you tell me?'

'The poison she took was certainly enough to kill her, and if she'd taken it a few hours earlier, she'd undoubtedly have been dead by the time the home help – Hallelujah Winifred – arrived.' The doctor paused. 'Have you had dealings with Mrs Brown before?'

'We've met,' Meadows said. 'Why do you ask?'

'From the state her joints are in, I would say that even going from the bedroom to the toilet would be a huge and painful effort for her. On the other hand, I've read reports of cases in which women in a similar condition have somehow been able to walk for miles and miles. You don't think she's one of those cases, do you, detective sergeant?'

'Definitely not,' Meadows said. 'I couldn't say for certain, but I'd be surprised if she'd left the house in years.'

'If that's the case, then she was definitely assisted in her suicide attempt, because whoever collected all the ingredients for the poison must have been reasonably fit.'

'Collected all the ingredients? Are you telling me the poison was home-made?'

'According to our toxicology department, there's no doubt about it. It has a belladonna base, but there are a couple of other ingredients which were obviously collected wild.'

'Do you think I could see her?' Meadows asked.

'If she agrees to see you, I've no objection,' the doctor said, 'but you'll probably get no more out of her than I did.'

Jed Slater was halfway through his pint of brown split when he saw DS Higgins enter the snug bar of the Old Brown Cow, and the plan of action which came immediately into his head was that he should pretend he'd never noticed the sergeant, and just hope that he'd go away.

The weakness of his strategy was revealed to him when Higgins walked right over to where he was sitting, and said, 'I want a word, Jed.'

Slater looked around him, as if he imagined that there was some other Jed sitting there, and when he found none, he said, 'You want a word with *me*, Mr Higgins?'

'That's right,' Higgins confirmed.

'Should I be asking for my lawyer?' Slater wondered.

Higgins grinned. 'Course not. We're on different sides of the fence, but we're still old mates, aren't we?'

'Mates' was the very last word Slater would have used to describe their relationship, but he felt it wisest to answer with a cautious, 'I suppose so.'

'So what's all this talk of lawyers, then? To tell you the truth, you've rather hurt my feelings.'

'What's on your mind, Mr Higgins?' Jed Slater asked, giving in to the inevitable.

DS Higgins looked around him. 'I'll be honest with you, Jed, I'm not entirely comfortable with the idea of having our little chat here, where there's all these criminals who might listen in. I think that we should go somewhere a little more private.'

'Like where?'

'Like the backyard.'

'I'd rather not do that, Mr Higgins.'

The sergeant frowned. 'Well, of course, if you'd prefer to put it on a formal footing, we could always go down to the station.'

Jed Slater sighed heavily. 'All right, Mr Higgins,' he agreed, 'the backyard it is.'

With considerable misgivings, Slater followed Higgins into the enclosed backyard.

Midway between the toilets and the towers of empty beer crates, Higgins came to a halt and turned to face Slater.

'It's like this, Jed,' he said, 'I've really not got time for any pissing about on this particular case, so what I need are straight answers to straight questions. Have you got that?'

'Yes, Mr Higgins,' Slater agreed, worriedly.

'Back in the good old days, when I was on the beat, you were a cat burglar – and a good one, if I may say so, a regular drainpipe artist.' Higgins paused. 'So what happened?'

'I don't know what you mean, Mr Higgins.'

'Did you decide it was a young man's game, and it would be best to move on? Is that why you became a motorbike thief?'

'I'm not a—' Slater began.

Then, as Higgins sank his fist into Slater's stomach, Slater gasped with pain and sank to his knees.

'You see, that's the sort of thing I'm talking about when I say I can't afford to be pissed about,' Higgins said. 'And what does all that lead to? You're making me *hurt* you – and that's really the last thing I want to do.'

'This is police brutality,' Slater groaned.

'No, you've got that wrong, Jed,' Higgins told him, lashing out with his left foot. '*This* is police brutality.'

Higgins kicked him again, then reached down and pulled him into an upright position.

'And *this* is police brutality,' he said, lifting Slater off his feet and flinging him across the yard.

Slater's body slammed hard into the towers of beer crates, and several of the crates toppled over, landing on his body in the two or three seconds after he hit the ground.

The noise of crashing crates and breaking glass brought several of the customers rushing to the back door.

'Get back inside!' said Higgins in a voice which left no room for discussion. 'Do it now!'

The men retreated into the pub, and Higgins strolled over to where Slater was lying.

'Let's start again,' he suggested, 'only this time, let's cut out all the small talk and go right to the heart of the matter. A few months ago, you bought a set of dodgy licence plates from my old mate Frank Brough, and you put them on a 250cc Honda that you'd stolen from God knows where. Now here's my question for you, Jed. Who did you sell that bike to?'

'Barry Hodges,' Slater said – and tiny bubbles of blood formed around his mouth as he spoke.

'I really do hope you have an address for this Barry Hodges of yours?' Higgins said.

'No!'

'That's the wrong answer, son. I may just have to knock you about a bit more.'

'But I do know where he works,' Slater said hastily.

'And where might that be?'

'At the Big-Buy supermarket on Preston New Road. He's got a job in their warehouse.'

Higgins reached down, grabbed Slater by the lapels of his jacket, and hauled him to his feet.

'Think you can stand without support?' he asked, and when Slater nodded, he released his hold on one of the lapels, and used the hand thus freed to brush down the other man's front.

'You're a real mess, Jed,' he said as he worked. 'If I was you, I'd go to the toilet and freshen up a bit before I went back into the pub.' He continued brushing. 'I'm going to let you get away with nicking that motorbike, even if you did confess. Say thank you.'

'Thank you,' Slater mumbled.

'But if I hear even a whisper that you've been saying I employed undue force, I'll be coming for you. Understood?'

'Understood,' Slater said.

Higgins let go of the other man completely, reached into his pocket, and came out with a five-pound note.

'There you are,' he said, sliding it into Slater's top pocket. 'Why don't you have a drink on me?'

As the bus was pulling up at the stop which was directly opposite the crematorium, Louisa noticed that there were perhaps a dozen men, most of them holding cameras, standing at the entrance to the building.

She pointed them out to John Green.

'The second we get off the bus, they'll descend on us like a pack of hounds,' she said.

'What if we ask them to go away?' John Green asked.

'They won't.'

'Not even if I appeal to their sense of decency?'

'They're not paid to have a sense of decency – they're paid to bring home the story.'

'So what should I do?'

'There's only one thing you can do – and that's ignore them. Look straight ahead, as if they weren't even there, and – most importantly – keep moving whatever they say to you.'

'Crematorium!' the bus driver called out. 'This is the crematorium.'

'You're so much wiser than I am – so much better at dealing with the world,' John said, as he stood up.

'That's only because I'm used to seeing my mum do this sort of thing,' Louisa said, taking his hand and giving it a comforting squeeze.

She'd not thought of her mum for at least half an hour, but now she did, it was hard not to start crying.

As Louisa had predicted, the reporters ran towards them, firing questions as they did so.

'How do you feel, John?'

'Do you think the police are doing enough, John?'

'Is there anything you'd like to say to the great British public?'

Louisa took John's hand.

'Let's go,' she said.

The reporters knew better than to try and block their way, and instead they formed an unwelcome escort, some of them flanking Louisa, the rest flanking John.

And, all the time, the questions kept raining down.

'Are you his girlfriend?'

'What's your name, love?'

'Did you know Mary?'

And then they were safe inside the crematorium, and the reporters were still outside, acting very much like the baying pack of hounds that Louisa had compared them to earlier.

A middle-aged porter in a grey suit was waiting for them as they entered the building.

'Are you family or friends of the late Mary Green?' he asked, in a sympathetic voice.

'Yes,' Louisa said, since John seemed incapable of words.

'Then follow me, please.'

The porter led them into a room which could have been called a chapel if you wanted to call it a chapel, but might have just passed as a very formal waiting room if you had no religious inclinations. There was seating for perhaps a hundred people, but none of the seats were taken.

'Time wise, it's getting rather close to the ceremony. Will there be anyone else coming?' the porter asked.

John shook his head.

'What, no one at all?' the porter asked, amazed.

'You heard him,' Louisa snapped angrily. 'There won't be anyone else coming.'

But she was soon proved wrong. A tall square man – looking very uncomfortable in a formal black suit – entered almost as soon as she'd spoken, and nodded to them.

'Do you know who he is?' John asked Louisa, and though there were no notices on the wall which said you had to speak in a whisper, speak in a whisper was what he did. 'The way he glanced across here, just now, it certainly seems as if he knows you.'

'He's my Uncle Colin,' Louisa admitted.

'And what's he doing here?'

'He's a detective inspector.'

'I still don't see why he should be here.'

'The police always attend the funerals of murder victims. There will be more plain clothes officers outside.'

'But why?'

'You don't want to know,' Louisa said.

'Yes, I do,' John Green insisted.

'The murderer will often turn up at the funeral,' Louisa said, speaking quickly, as if she couldn't wait to be free of the words.

'No!' John gasped. 'That simply can't be true!'

'It is.'

'But that's disgusting – that's . . . obscene.'

'Murder's never a pleasant business,' Louisa said.

It was something she had heard her mother say many times, and she was merely (if unconsciously) imitating her, but the moment she'd spoken, she realized that these were not the words you should ever say to the brother of a victim, and she looked down at the floor, wishing it would open up and swallow her.

ELEVEN

Mrs Brown was no longer on the intensive care ward, though she was still attached to a number of tubes and drips. She looked exhausted, Meadows thought, but then anyone who'd been hauled back from the very threshold of death was bound to be showing the effects.

'I know you,' the old woman said. 'You're that policewoman who came to see me in Sebastopol Street.'

'That's right, I am,' Meadows agreed.

'I won't answer any questions,' Mrs Brown said, 'so if that's what you're here for, you can leave right now.'

'I won't *ask* you any questions,' Meadows said, pulling up a chair. 'I just thought you might appreciate the company.'

'I'm not sorry I'm alive, you know,' the old woman told her. 'I know I should be, but I'm not.'

'You very nearly weren't,' Meadows said.

'I waited too long before taking the poison,' Mrs Brown said. 'It wasn't that I was frightened of the act of dying – I just thought that God would never forgive me for taking my own life.'

'But eventually, you managed to persuade yourself that He would,' Meadows said softly.

'No, I realized that whatever God felt about it, my first duty was to the others,' Mrs Brown told her. She looked out of the window, and then back at Meadows. 'You want me to tell you who the others are, don't you?' she added, in an accusatory tone. 'That's why you're here.'

'I'm here to keep you company,' Meadows said. 'I'm here to listen to whatever you want to tell me, and no more.'

Mrs Brown fell silent, and Meadows wondered if she'd blown it, then the old woman said, 'Are you married?'

'No,' Meadows said.

Not any more, she thought to herself.

'Have you ever *been* married?' Mrs Brown asked.

'No,' Meadows said – because when you were conducting conversations which were really interrogations, it was best not to complicate matters with an inconvenient truth.

'Have you ever been in love, then?' Mrs Brown asked.

'No,' Meadows replied – and on this question, at least, she was being entirely truthful.

'I was in love once,' Mrs Brown said wistfully. 'None of us were supposed to be – we were supposed to put duty first, second and third, but I simply couldn't help myself.'

'What happened to him?' Meadows asked.

'The whole thing was doomed from the start. He was an outsider, you see, and we can never marry outsiders.'

'So you married Mr Brown instead?'

'Yes. Arthur was a good husband to me – I couldn't fault him in any way – but there was never any spark between us, and on the day that he died, all I could feel was relief that I wouldn't have to put up with him any longer.'

'Well, at least you'd experienced real love, if only for a short time,' Meadows said.

'Yes, but in some ways, that only made it worse, you see,' Mrs Brown said. 'None of the others had ever been in love, so they didn't know what they were missing. But I did.' She sighed. 'We're brought up to love God and to serve Him dutifully, but there have been times, over the last few years, when I've found myself wondering if He really loves us in return.'

'What makes you wonder that?' Meadows asked.

'Well, if He truly cared for us, wouldn't He want us to have at least a *little* joy in our lives? And I began to wonder if we've always been right about everything, as we're always told we've been by the Trus . . .'

'By the Trus . . .?' Meadows repeated.

'Of course, if we *have* been right, then what we've done has been a truly glorious thing and worth all the sacrifices,' Mrs Brown said, avoiding the implied question. 'But what if we've not been right about it? What if we've got the whole thing horribly wrong? Then everything has been such a waste . . . such a terrible, terrible waste.'

'Mary often left you alone on Sunday afternoons, didn't she?' Meadows asked.

'Yes, she went off with her boyfriend. He picked her up on his motorcycle – and when she came back from seeing him, she was so happy.'

'But he's an outsider?'

'Yes.'

'What did you think would happen in the end?'

'I thought she might leave. I thought she might be brave enough to do something that I was too frightened to do.'

It was time for the big one, Meadows thought.

'Who do you think killed her?' she asked.

'It could have been the boyfriend,' Mrs Brown said.

'Why would he have done it?'

Mrs Brown's eyes became both dreamy and tearful.

'When I told my one true love that I couldn't see him anymore, he started to cry,' Mrs Brown said, 'but there was a moment, before the tears came, when I'm sure he wanted to kill me. And perhaps that's what happened with Mary.'

'But you think there might be another possibility, don't you?' Meadows sensed.

'It is not our place to question the way that things are,' Mrs Brown said. 'It is not our place to *do* anything. We are sources of the light, and that should be enough for us.'

'What do you mean – sources of the light?' Meadows asked.

'I can't tell you that. And even if I could, you either wouldn't believe or wouldn't understand.'

'I'm sorry, I interrupted you,' Meadows said.

'It is because we each only play our own little part that we know nothing of the grand design,' the old woman said. 'But there are those who know – those who have been given the power to protect us when we come under attack.'

'You think your own people may have killed her,' Meadows said, though she had no idea who Mrs Brown's 'people' might be.

'Perhaps it's all part of the great plan,' Mrs Brown said. 'My life was to be sacrificed for the greater good, wasn't it – that's why he brought me the poison. And maybe he decided that Mary had to be sacrificed, too.'

Another official, looking grave and dignified, approached Louisa and John Green in a sedate – almost stately – manner.

'Are you ready to start?' he asked, and when neither of them answered, the professional veneer of solemnity cracked a little, and he added, in a much crisper, more businesslike tone, 'We can give you another five minutes, if you really need it, but this is a busy day for us, and any longer than that . . .'

'We're ready to start,' Louisa said.

Two more solemn-looking men entered, guiding a trolley with the coffin on it. With practiced ease, they slid the coffin onto what looked like an altar, but was in fact a conveyor belt.

The men with the trolley withdrew, and the grave and dignified official said, 'I understand there is to be no formal ceremony, but would either of you like to say a few words?'

Louisa experienced a wave of panic.

If John asked her to say a few words, what on earth *could* she say? she wondered.

Yes, they had been fellow members of the Upper Sixth, and had probably seen each other every day, but unlike her brother, Mary had never come into the sixth form common room during her free periods. She had been Mary the Quiet – Mary the Mouse – a grey presence which drifted through life without seeming to touch or affect anyone else.

But how could she say that, when the dead girl was lying only feet away from her? How could she send Mary off on the journey from which no one returned with such bland nothingness?

'My sister was a quiet girl who most people never really got to understand,' John said, speaking as though he was addressing a full chapel rather than just a policeman and a girl from school who was, in truth, little more than an acquaintance. 'She was never going to change the world,' he continued, 'but I loved her. I don't think she ever knew how much I loved her – in fact, I know she didn't – and now she never will.'

It was obvious that he had finished – was incapable of saying any more. The official made a slight gesture which some hidden observer saw, and the conveyor belt began to roll.

'I need . . . I need to sit down for a minute,' John said.

'Of course you do,' Louisa agreed, ushering him to one of the pews.

She looked across the room at Beresford, and made a sweeping gesture with her hands. He nodded, to show that he had understood, and left the room.

'I'm ready to leave now,' John said, standing up.

'All right,' Louisa agreed. 'But I think we should wait in the foyer for a few minutes more before we go.'

It was good to be at work, Barry Hodges thought. Carrying out operations he'd carried out hundreds of times before – and joking with the lads between times – it was almost possible to believe that life had settled back into its normal pattern. Of course, he'd seen his bike – and himself – on the lunchtime news, yet somehow that seemed to have no relevance at all to him as he was now.

Even if he was arrested, he told himself, as he steered his forklift truck along the narrow canyon which ran between the mountains of stacked boxes containing baked beans and tinned peas, it wasn't the end of the world. He'd been arrested often enough in the past to appreciate that there was a big difference between what the police knew, and what the police could prove – and the trick was to ignore their assurances that they had enough to put him away, and just keep denying everything.

As he turned out of the canyon, he saw his supervisor signalling him to stop the truck.

'The big boss wants to see you in his office,' the supervisor said.

'Any idea what it's about?' Hodges asked.

'Yes, apparently one of the other workers has made a complaint about you,' the supervisor said.

'Who was it?'

'I don't know, and if I did know, I wouldn't tell you.'

It would be Roy Meres, Hodges thought – it was bound to be. Ever since he'd stuck the lad's head down the toilet and flushed, the little arsehole had had it in for him. That was the trouble with fellers like Meres – they had absolutely no sense of humour.

'When does the boss want to see me?' Hodges asked.

'I asked him that,' the supervisor replied, 'and he said, "How does *immediately* sound?".'

Hodges climbed down from the truck, and walked in the direction of the office.

If it was Meres who'd complained, he decided, he'd invent something that the other lad had done to him to justify the head down the bog routine. Yes, that shouldn't be too difficult.

He knocked on the warehouse manager's door, and a voice from inside said, 'Come in.'

The manager was standing with his back to the door, next to the filing cabinet. He was wearing the same long khaki work coat he always wore over his suit, but that day, there seemed to be something wrong with it.

It was as Hodges finally worked out that what was wrong was that the manager's coat was too small for the man who was actually wearing it, that DS Higgins swung round to face him.

'Well, hello Barry Hodges,' he said, with a broad smile spread across his face. 'You, my son, are nicked.'

Hodges turned around, only to discover that the doorway was blocked by two uniformed constables, who seemed to have appeared from nowhere.

When Louisa and John Green stepped out of the crematorium and into the bright sunlight, there was no sign of the reporters.

'Where have they gone?' John asked.

'You sound as if you're disappointed they're not still here,' Louisa said, with a little laugh. 'Oh God,' she moaned, 'I'm sorry.'

'The fact that we've just said goodbye to my sister doesn't mean we can never laugh again,' John said. 'And it did sound as if I was complaining they weren't here, which *would have been* quite funny, I suppose.' He paused. 'I really wasn't complaining, you know.'

'I know you weren't.'

'So what did happen to the reporters?'

'My Uncle Colin will have got rid of them.'

'Why would he have done that?'

'Because I asked him to.'

John Green looked horrified. 'He didn't . . . he surely didn't . . .?'

Louisa laughed again – and this time, she felt better about it.

'What are you imagining?' she asked. 'That a couple of black police vans will have swooped down, and big burly constables waving their truncheons in a menacing manner will have forced the cowering reporters into the backs of the vans, as if they were no more than cattle?'

'Well, not exactly that, I suppose, but they are . . . you know . . . gone,' John said.

'Uncle Colin will have had a quiet word with them,' Louisa said. 'He will have said that I'm his niece, and so he'd appreciate it, as a personal favour, if they'd leave me alone. He will have hinted that when he has some really juicy information to hand out, he'll remember their act of kindness, and see that they get it first. And he will have suggested – ever so subtly – that if they don't do as he wishes, they will suddenly become invisible around police headquarters.'

John laughed. 'That's the second time in one afternoon you've made me feel like a naïve child,' he said.

'I didn't mean to—' Louisa began.

'I don't mind,' John interrupted her. 'I've been carrying the burden for so long, it's a great relief to let it rest on someone else for a while.'

'So what do we do now?' Louisa asked.

'Well, if there was a wake, we could go to that,' John said, almost lightheartedly. 'But there isn't one.' He paused for a moment. 'I know! Let's go and see your mother!'

'Oh no, John, I couldn't possibly impose on you to go and see her,' Louisa said.

'Why not?' John Green asked. 'You've been supporting me all afternoon, it's only fair that I give you a little support in return.'

TWELVE

Barry Hodges sat sullenly at the table in Interview Room B, with his solicitor – a man who looked every bit the part, with his half-moon glasses and blue pinstriped suit – by his side.

The solicitor's name was Andrew Selby, and it was a pity they'd drawn him, DS Higgins thought, because unlike many legal aid solicitors, he would generally go the extra mile for his client. Still, you had to play the hand you were dealt, he told himself as he made a great show of flicking through Hodges' file, pausing occasionally to tut-tut.

'You really have been a bit of a naughty boy, haven't you, Barry?' the sergeant asked.

'No comment,' Hodges replied.

'None invited,' Higgins told him, 'it was a purely rhetorical question.' He turned to the solicitor. 'Would you like to explain to your client what rhetorical means?'

'It means that Sergeant Higgins is doing his best to undermine your self-confidence by making you look and feel stupid,' Selby said smoothly. 'It means he's trying to get you to believe that you'll never win against him, so you might as well just give up now, and say whatever it is that he wants you to say – whether or not it happens to be true.'

Mistake! Higgins thought. I've just made a bloody big mistake by inviting Selby into the interrogation.

'That's not what it means at all, Mr Selby,' he told the solicitor, doing his best to hide his anger.

'You may well be right, on a purely linguistic level,' Selby said calmly. 'Nevertheless, that is how I have chosen to interpret it within the dynamics of an interrogation.'

And now – bloody idiot that I am – I've only made matters worse, Higgins told himself.

'It's your temper that always lets you down, isn't it, Barry?' he said, shifting his focus back onto the suspect, in an attempt to recapture some of the ground that he'd lost. 'You just can't help getting into fights when you think somebody is trying to take the piss out of you – and it seems as if virtually everybody you meet wants to do just that.'

'There's a lot of shitheads about,' Barry Hodges said, 'and I've never hit anybody who didn't hit me back.'

'True,' Higgins agreed. 'Of course, they wouldn't have needed to hit you back if you hadn't hit them in the first place. But you're right, in a way – the fact that they did hit you back is probably what's kept you out of prison. It hasn't kept you completely out of trouble, though, has it? And if you're wondering what makes me say that – not that you should be – it's because, according to what it says here in your record, you still have two years of a probation sentence to serve.'

Hodges kept silent.

'I said you still have two years of a probation sentence to serve, don't you?' Higgins repeated, with a new harshness to his voice.

'Yes,' Barry Hodges admitted.

Good, Higgins thought, making the little bastard admit it was the first step in regaining some of his authority.

'I'm glad we're both clear on that, Barry,' he said, in a much softer tone. 'You know that you really are in big trouble, don't you?'

Hodges said nothing.

'But if you work with me, I promise I'll work with you, and together, we'll find a way out of this mess,' Higgins said.

Hodges maintained his silence.

'I mean, when you look at it from a slightly different perspective, it was probably just as much her fault as it was yours,' Higgins said. 'She was a bit of a prick teaser and—'

'I don't know what you're talking about,' Hodges interrupted. 'Who was a bit of a prick teaser?'

'Who? Why, the girl who was killed in Backend Woods last Sunday, of course.'

'She was nothing to do with me.'

Higgins sighed. 'You're on video tape, driving through the main gate, with her sitting right behind you.'

'Are you talking about the tape they showed on the television?'

'That's right.'

'That feller was wearing a full-face helmet. It could have been me, but it could have been you, as well. It could even have been Mr Selby.'

'Mr Selby and I are the wrong body shape,' Higgins said.

'You don't even know the girl on the bike was the one what got done in the woods – because she was wearing a helmet, too.'

'The fact of the matter is, that's your bike on the tape,' Higgins said, returning to the one thing he knew he could prove.

'But it isn't my bike at all,' Hodges said. 'It was – until last Saturday – but then I sold it.'

'Who to?'

'To a man I met in the back room of the Black Horse.'

'What was his name, this man?'

'Bob.'

'What was his surname?'

'I don't know. He didn't say, and I didn't ask.'

'Describe him to me.'

'He was just like any other feller you might meet on the street.'

'What colour was his hair?'

'Brown.'

'How tall was he?'

'Average height.'

'How was he built?'

'Average build.'

'What about his nose?'

'He had one.'

'You're lying to me, Barry,' Higgins said. 'And do you know how I know you're lying? I know because if this man really did exist, and if you really did sell the bike to him, then you would have had to put his name – his full name – in the log book.'

There was no log book, of course, but Hodges wouldn't want to admit that, for obvious reasons, Higgins thought.

'There was no log book,' Hodges said, confounding expectation.

'Every bike has a log book,' Higgins said. 'It has to. It's the law.'

'This one didn't – because it was stolen.'

'So you admit to buying *stolen property,* do you?'

'Yes.'

'And then selling it again?'

'Yes.'

Criminals could often be led into accidently confessing to a major crime in their efforts to avoid being charged with a lesser one, but, contrary to appearances, Hodges was obviously too smart for that, and was doing just the opposite.

Higgins wondered whether or not now was the right time to introduce the picnic basket. If he could have tied it directly to Hodges, there would have been nothing to consider, but unfortunately, his prints – if they *were* on the basket – were blurred beyond identification. Still, there was no way that Hodges could know that, and it might be worth taking the risk.

'We've found a wicker picnic basket, Barry,' he said. 'It has your prints all over it.'

For a second, Hodges looked gobsmacked, then he smiled and said, 'It must be my picnic basket, then, mustn't it?'

'So what was it doing in Backend Woods?'

'I don't know. Maybe the feller that I sold it to took it there.'

'What feller?'

'The same one I sold the bike to.' Hodges clicked his fingers as if a brilliant idea had just occurred to him. 'It must have been the feller I sold the bike to that you can see on the video,' he said. 'He must be the one that did the girl.'

The whole story was clearly ridiculous, Higgins thought, and no police officer worth his salt would accept it for a second. The lack of fingerprints on the picnic hamper raised a few awkward questions, it was true, but that was nothing that couldn't be got round with a little creative thinking.

But he didn't feel he could arrest Hodges for the murder yet, because it seemed unlikely that – on the evidence he had so far – the chief constable would be prepared to instigate a prosecution.

Sod it, then, he thought. It had been a bloody long day, and he might as well just charge the little toerag with dealing in stolen property – which was enough to keep him locked up overnight – then go to the nearest pub and get smashed out of his head.

John Green and Louisa stood at the side of the hospital bed, looking down at Monika Paniatowski.

Her mother had always been pale, Louisa thought – she was, after all, a Northern European, born far from the Mediterranean – but now her face was so white it was almost like candle wax.

Was candle wax what they made death masks out of? she caught herself wondering.

Oh God, how could you even *think* that? she asked herself.

But it didn't matter if she thought it, did it? It didn't matter if death masks were never off her mind – because her mum *wasn't going to die*!

'Hello, Mum,' she said.

What next? she thought. What did you say to a woman who was unconscious and might not even be able to hear you?

You couldn't talk about the weather, because, shut up in this room as she was, the weather was of no interest to her.

You couldn't ask what she'd been doing – because the only thing she'd been doing was not dying (at least for the moment).

She felt helpless. She felt useless. And she knew that any moment now, she was going to burst into tears, which was just about the worst thing she could possibly do.

And then John took her hand in his, and gave it a squeeze, and she felt her strength and confidence returning.

'I've got John with me here,' she said. 'John Green. You know him, don't you?'

'No, she doesn't know me,' John mouthed almost silently at her – though, as in the crematorium, there was probably no need to be quiet. 'We've never actually met.'

'We've just been to John's sister's cremation,' Louisa said. 'What made it extra sad was that we were the only ones there – except for Uncle Colin, of course, but he only came because he was a policeman.'

'Louisa's been a tower of strength to me, Ms Paniatowski,' John said. 'I don't know how I'd ever have managed without her.'

'She moved!' Louisa said excitedly. 'I swear her eyelid moved. Didn't you see it?'

'No, I don't think I did . . .'

'Say something else.'

'Like what? I can't think what to say.'

'Say anything!'

'Mary had a little lamb, its fleece was white as snow, and everywhere that Mary went, that lamb was sure to go.'

'Did you see it that time?' Louisa asked excitedly. 'Did you see the eye move?'

'Err yes, I think I did.'

Later, as they were leaving the hospital, John said, 'I feel such a fool for reciting a nursery rhyme, but my mind seemed to go into a panic, and I couldn't think of anything else.'

'You could have been reading the telephone directory for all it mattered,' Louisa said. 'The fact is, it seems to have done the trick.' She paused. 'Oh, I know it didn't seem much, but if she's just a little better tomorrow, and then a little better the day after that, she'll be back on her feet before any of us realizes it.'

THIRTEEN

B eresford, Meadows and Crane were sitting at their usual table in the Drum and Monkey. They were sitting further apart than usual, as if to disguise the fact that someone was missing – but if anything, it only seemed to emphasize Monika Paniatowski's absence.

'I screwed up,' Crane said miserably.

'We all screwed up,' Beresford told him, 'each and every one of us – and if the boss had been here, she would have screwed up, too.'

But would she? he wondered. Would she really?

'I think I've got the general idea, but, if you don't mind, I'd like to hear the specific details,' Meadows said.

'Two of the three boys who spent Sunday with Roger Smith – supposedly playing Diplomacy – have vanished into thin air,' Crane said. 'And it's not just the boys who have vanished – their whole families have gone.'

'You're sure of this, are you?' Beresford asked.

Crane nodded. 'I went round to their houses, and when nobody answered the door, I had a word with the neighbours. All most of them could say was that they hadn't seen any movement this morning, but there were a couple of old dears with bladder problems who said that they saw a black van at around two o'clock this morning.'

'Was it a furniture van?' Beresford asked.

'No, it was much smaller than that. From what the witnesses said, I think it was probably a Ford Transit.'

'So they didn't take any furniture with them?'

'No, it looked as if they had one suitcase each, and that was it.'

'So what did you do next?'

'I went back to the school, and asked if any other family had

failed to turn up en masse. There were two more, and when I went
to *their* houses, I found that they'd disappeared as well.'

'And that's just from one school,' Meadows said. 'It's possible
there are more of them, isn't it?'

'I'm bloody certain there are more of them,' Crane said.
'Anyway, I've started building up a profile of the missing families.
I've not had much time, so it's far from complete, but I've already
found some striking similarities between them.'

'Like what?' Meadows asked.

'None of the mothers worked outside the house, which, in this
day and age – and especially in Lancashire, where there's a tradi-
tion of women having jobs – is a rare thing. The fathers *appeared*
to work, but none of the neighbours could tell me *where* they
worked.'

'So what?' Meadows asked.

'Again, this is *Lancashire*,' Beresford said. 'Everybody in a
neighbourhood normally knows what everybody else does, and if
Jack had asked those people on that street what any of their *other*
neighbours did for a living, they'd have been able to tell him right
away.'

'Are we trying to find out if any of them really *did* have jobs?'
Meadows asked.

'Yes,' Beresford said. 'We've contacted social security, and the
Inland Revenue, but God knows how long it will take those paper
shufflers to come up with any answers.' He paused to light a
cigarette. 'What else do we know about these families, Jack?'

'The pastoral care department at the school was understandably
very cagey about telling me too much, but from the few hints they
were willing to drop, I think I've been able to build up some sort
of a picture,' Crane said. 'Michael Gray, Philip Jones and John
Green – the three lads who spent Sunday at Roger Smith's house
– are all pretty good students with a positive attitude and outgoing
personalities. The other children in the cult, however—'

'Wait a minute, Jack,' Beresford said, 'when did we decide to
start calling it a cult?'

'What else would we call it?' Crane asked.

'Fair point,' Beresford conceded.

'The other children who are members of the cult – and that
includes Mary Green, the dead girl – don't do anything like as

well. Their main ambition seems to be just get by – and no more. And all of them – and again, significantly, this includes Mary Green – are complete loners.'

'You mean they don't mix with the rest of the kids in their class?' Beresford asked.

'I mean they don't even mix with *each other*. And it's the same at home. We know that the Grays and the Joneses are members of the cult, yet – according to the neighbours again – neither family ever visited the other. In fact, neither family *ever* had visitors. And it goes beyond that. Mr Gray never drops in at the local pub, even though it's just on the corner, and when Mr Jones was invited to join the committee which was organizing the street party to celebrate the queen's silver jubilee, he turned it down flat.'

'And why do you think that is?' Beresford asked.

'It beats me,' Crane admitted. 'Most cults are quite open about themselves. They're eager to recruit new members, because that's how they survive. But this cult's main aim in life seems to have been to hide the fact that it even existed, almost to the point at which it seems driven by very little else. But why belong to a cult that does nothing – a cult in which the members never even seem to get together?'

'So maybe you're wrong about them being a cult at all,' Beresford suggested. 'Maybe what you've uncovered isn't the clear evidence you seem to think it is, but just a series of coincidences that—'

'They didn't just *leave* Whitebridge at the same time,' Crane interrupted, 'they *arrived* at the same time. Five years ago, none of these people lived in the town – and then, suddenly, they *all* did.'

Beresford did still not seem convinced. 'I wonder if we're only taking this so seriously because we need to feel we're doing *something* positive,' he said. 'And I wonder if perhaps it's not just a waste of our time. DS Higgins has the motorbike rider in custody, and is convinced that he's our killer.'

'Yes, Higgins does have the man in custody, but only because he was pointed in that direction by the work Jack did,' Meadows said, with a hint of indignation. 'But there are holes in the case he's trying to build up that you could drive a double-decker bus through.'

'Like what?' Beresford asked.

'Barry Hodges' fingerprints aren't on the picnic basket, for a start. Now, if he is the killer, how is that even remotely possible? When he says he sold the bike on Saturday night, can we say for certain that isn't true? Maybe he just lent the killer the bike for the day, and is now too scared to admit it.'

'How do you know his fingerprints aren't on the basket, and that he says he sold the bike?' asked Beresford, who, until that moment, had believed that DS Higgins was playing his cards very close to his chest.

'I have my sources,' Meadows said, enigmatically.

Of course she did, Beresford thought – and no doubt the particular policeman who'd given her this information, had once whipped her, or allowed her to whip him – or whatever else it was these weird people did behind closed doors.

'All right, we'll stick with it for a while longer,' Beresford said. 'Am I right in assuming that you both have theories revolving around this idea of a cult?'

'You are,' Crane agreed.

'Then let's hear them.'

'I'll go first, because my theory's shorter and far less compli-cated,' Meadows said. 'Actually, it's not really *my* theory at all. It was Mrs Brown who came up with it. She thinks that one of the members of the cult killed Mary Green. I suspect, though she didn't say in so many words, that she thinks Roger Smith is the murderer.'

'And why would Roger Smith have killed her?' Beresford asked.

'He'd have killed her because she broke one of the cardinal rules of the cult, by having a relationship – every Sunday afternoon – with someone who wasn't a member.'

'All right,' Beresford said, 'so what's your theory, Jack?'

'The killer washed her vagina out with tea, but everyone involved in the investigation seems to want to overlook that,' Crane said. 'And *why* do they want to overlook it?'

'Because it doesn't seem to lead anywhere?' Beresford asked.

'Because if you accept it as part of a ritual – and what else could it possibly be? – then all these theories about revenge killings and punishment killings completely collapse.'

'So you think it's a ritual killing?'

'Yes.'

'What kind of ritual killing?'

'I couldn't say, exactly, but I've been looking at some possibilities. Ritual killings, it seems to me, are often an attempt to come to terms with outside forces, either by neutralizing them or propitiating them.'

'Stop right there,' Beresford said, holding up his hand. 'Don't say any more until I've been away and got myself a degree in anthropology.'

Crane grinned. 'You'd like me to keep it simple,' he said.

'I'd like you to keep it *very* simple,' Beresford replied.

'There's this tribe in Papua New Guinea who have had very little contact with the outside world,' Crane said, 'but once every three years, they send a girl to the copper mines, which are a few miles away from the tribal area. The girl stays at the copper mine for three days, during which time she'll sleep with any man who wants to sleep with her. It is, most anthropologists think, a ritual-ized bribe to the copper company to leave them – and their way of life – alone. Anyway, at the end of the three days, she returns to the tribe. Once there, she's purified with sacred oils – and then she disappears forever.'

'They kill her,' Meadows said.

'That seems more than likely,' Crane agreed.

'Mary was still a virgin,' Beresford pointed out.

Crane suppressed a sigh. Beresford was a bloody good bobby, he thought – probably better than he'd ever be himself – but he did have his limitations.

'I'm not drawing an exact parallel, sir,' he said. 'Papua is a very different country to England – it's estimated that 55% of the women there have been forced to have sex against their will – but I think that the cult in Whitebridge, whatever it's based on, may have been enacting some kind of ritual which would lead them, inevitably, to killing Mary.'

'It's a push,' Beresford said.

'It's a push that a cult with no apparent purpose should set itself up in Whitebridge at all – but that's what seems to have happened,' Crane said. He took a slug of his best bitter. 'With your permis-sion, sir, I'd like to call in an expert,' he continued.

'An expert? On what?'

'On cults.'

'I can't see the chief constable agreeing to pay someone like that,' Beresford said dubiously.

'He doesn't have to,' Crane replied. 'George Oppenheimer won't want paying. He probably won't even want his expenses covering. He's an Oxford don, and if I know him as well as I think I do, I'm sure he'll jump at the chance to examine our evidence.'

'All right, it can't do any harm to get in touch with him, can it?' Beresford asked. He looked down at his watch. 'We'll talk to the Greens first thing in the morning, and see if we can get anything new from them,' he continued. 'But before we call it a night, there's one more thing we need to deal with – Louisa was at Mary Green's funeral with John Green.'

'Do you mean there *as well* as John Green, or there *with him*?' Meadows asked.

'Very much *with him*,' Beresford said.

'And you didn't do anything about it?' Meadows asked.

'It's not an easy thing to do – create a scene at a funeral,' Beresford said, uncomfortably. 'Besides, we didn't know as much about the whole cult thing then as we do now.'

'You're going to have to talk to her,' Meadows said.

'The thing is,' Beresford replied, 'I thought it might sound better if it came from you.'

'Me!'

'Yes, you're a woman, like Monika—'

'I am not a woman like Monika at all,' Meadows said angrily. 'She's responsible and hard-working. She's a loving mother. I'm a couldn't-care-less, thrill-seeking, sado-masochistic aristocrat who—'

'Did you say "aristocrat" just then?' Crane asked.

'Yes, well, when compared to you lot, I'm almost bloody royalty. But you get the point about why I wouldn't be any good at talking to Louisa.'

'It has to be you,' Colin Beresford said. 'You know it does.'

'Yes,' Meadows admitted, with a heavy sigh, 'it probably does.'

They were sitting on the top deck of a double-decker bus when Louisa felt she must ask the question she'd been bursting to ask.

'Back in the hospital, you said you saw a change in my mother's expression,' she said. 'Did you really?'

'Yes,' John Green said.

And yet he was somehow failing to convince her.

'Be honest with me,' she pleaded, 'did you really see a change in my mum's expression?'

John looked down at the floor.

'No, I didn't,' he admitted.

'This is my stop,' Louisa said, getting up and ringing the bell. 'I'll see you in school.'

She stood up, and as she climbed down the stairs, she was aware that he was following her.

They both stepped off the platform, and the bus pulled away.

They stood watching it until it turned the corner, then John said, 'This isn't really your stop, is it?'

'So why did you say what you did about seeing my mother move?' she asked, almost in tears.

'Because it was what you wanted me to say,' he told her, 'and because it gave you hope.'

'I don't need false hope,' Louisa said bitterly.

'But hope is never false,' John said. 'It *can* never be false. Hope is a precious gift. With hope, we can change so many things – hope is a real power in the world, and with it by our side, we can defeat even the heaviest odds.' He took her arm. 'Come on, Louisa, I'll walk you home.'

They walked in silence until her house was in sight, then Louisa said, 'In school debates, you always start out by announcing that you're an atheist – but just then, you sounded almost like a Christian.'

'I am a Christian,' John said.

'Then why did you lie about it?'

'Because it was necessary – because that was what I had to do.'

'Who told you that you had to do things that way?'

'I can't discuss it,' John said. 'You just have to accept that my Christianity is, in many ways, different to yours.'

They had reached Louisa's front gate.

'Thank you for coming with me to my sister's funeral,' John said. 'I'll say goodnight now.'

She was not going to let him get away with that. Before he had time to turn, she put her arms around his neck and pulled his head down to her own level. And then, they were kissing.

John broke away.

'What's the matter?' Louisa asked, utterly bewildered at his reaction. 'Didn't you like it?'

'We shouldn't have done it,' he said, avoiding the question.

'Why not?' she asked.

'There's a danger of me becoming too fond of you,' he said.

'I think I am *already* very fond of you,' she told him.

'And as soon as I have permission from the police, I'll be leaving Whitebridge – and I won't ever be coming back.'

'Why?' she demanded.

He shrugged. 'Because that's the way it has to be. I have no right to a life of my own – no right to happiness – I have only duty.'

'No, you don't,' she said, 'nobody can make you do something you don't want to do.'

He smiled at her. 'You see, that's what you don't understand,' he said. 'The weight is crushing me, but I accept it gladly.'

He turned.

'Why not come inside?' she urged him.

'I've told you . . .'

'I'm not trying to deter you from your path, I'm just offering you – offering both of us – a little comfort before you go.'

He smiled again, more sadly this time. 'That would only make it harder,' he said.

And then he turned, and walked rapidly down the street.

FOURTEEN

B eresford was just unlocking the double deadlock bolt on his front door when he heard the phone start ringing in his living room.

'Shit!' he said.

It was more than likely, he thought, that the person calling him was one of that small select band of women who he had entrusted with his private number, and if it *was* one of them, she was more likely ringing him with a proposition he wouldn't want to refuse. But if she rang off before he got inside, then he would never know who'd called, and his chances of an evening of horizontal gymnastics – nature's way of easing away the tensions of the day – would be lost.

One more turn of the key, and the door was unlocked.

The phone was still ringing!

Oh, please, please don't hang up, he implored the unknown caller.

He dashed down the hallway and into his living room, and grabbed at the phone before it had a chance to fall silent on him.

'Colin Beresford,' he said.

'Get yourself over to the Greens' house as quick as you can,' a female voice said.

So he'd been right, it was a woman – but not one of the women he'd been expecting.

'The Greens?' he said. 'Which "Greens" are you talking about?'

'Don't piss me about, Shagger,' the woman said, 'there simply isn't time for that. I'm talking about the Greens who live on Balaclava Street – and you bloody well know I am.'

'Who is this?' Beresford asked.

'Just do it!' the woman said.

'How do I know this isn't a crank call?' Beresford said – although even as he was asking the question, he realized that it was unlikely a crank would have got her hands on his private number.

'You'll have to take my word for it being the real thing,' the woman said, 'and you'll be sorry if you don't.'

'If something *has* happened at the Greens' house, why haven't I been informed by police headquarters?' Beresford wondered, still with a little lingering suspicion.

The woman sighed, almost as if she despaired of him.

'You still don't get it, do you?' she asked – almost tauntingly. 'You haven't been informed because they've decided to cut you out of the loop.'

Behind her, Beresford heard a male voice say, 'You're wanted, boss,' and then the line went dead.

* * *

Meadows rang the doorbell, and it was Louisa who answered it.

She looked tired, Meadows thought, very, very tired.

'Do you mind if I come in?' she asked.

'No, I'd like that,' Louisa told her, smiling weakly.

They went into the cosy lounge.

'Would you like something to drink?' Louisa asked.

'No, I'm fine.'

They sat down, facing each other.

'Are the twins in bed?' Meadows asked.

'Yes.'

'What about Elena?'

'I gave her the night off. She's been under a lot of strain, you know.'

Gave her the night off, Meadows thought, hiding her smile. Louisa was becoming quite the little boss.

'I hear you went to Mary's funeral,' Meadows said.

The atmosphere in the room was suddenly almost chill.

'What you mean is that Uncle Colin told you I was at Mary's funeral,' Louisa said.

'Yes, I suppose that is what I mean,' Meadows conceded – and she was thinking, God, I'm hopeless at this sort of thing. 'Could I ask you *why* you were there?' she ploughed on.

'John asked me if I'd be willing to go with him, and I said I would,' Louisa answered, tight-lipped and defensive.

'It might be wise of you to steer a pretty wide berth of him from now on,' Meadows said.

'And why is that?'

'He's rather closely connected to the investigation.'

'Well, of course he is, because it was his sister that was killed. I'm rather close to the investigation, too, because my mother's in hospital, dangerously ill – so we've a lot in common, haven't we?'

'His connection is slightly more direct than that,' Kate Meadows said awkwardly.

'Are you telling me he's a suspect?'

'No, of course not – or, at least, no more than anyone on our radar could be a suspect.'

'So what is the problem?'

'I can't tell you that,' Meadows said.

'Isn't that just typical of an adult?' Louisa asked angrily. 'They tell you that you shouldn't do something because it will be bad for you, but they won't tell you *why* it will be bad for you? Well, that may work on kids, Kate, but – in case you haven't noticed – I'm not a kid anymore.'

'Of course you're not,' Meadows agreed, 'and it's not because I think of you as a kid that I can't tell you more – it's because you're a civilian.'

'I'm a bobby's daughter,' Louisa said. 'I haven't been a civilian since I learned to walk and talk.'

'All right,' Meadows said, 'maybe I can tell you a little more. We think that John belongs to some sort of cult, and—'

'He's a Christian!' Louisa exploded. 'I know that for people like you – people who don't believe in anything very much, thank you – having a faith doesn't really seem important, but I'm a Christian, too, and it means something to me.'

'I don't think he's your *kind* of Christian,' Meadows said.

'And that's why you've come round here tonight – not to see me, but to warn me off John, because he's not my kind of Christian? Well, you needn't have bothered, because I won't be seeing him again. But I'd hate you to think that's because you and Uncle Colin disapprove. I'd want to see him whatever you thought – I really would – and the reason we won't be seeing each other is because *he* doesn't think it's a good idea.'

'Be very careful who you give yourself to, Louisa,' Meadows said softly.

'Give myself to!' Louisa repeated. 'What a quaint way you have of expressing yourself.' Then, the full implications of the words hit her. 'You think I'm a virgin, don't you?' she practically screamed.

'I *know* you're a virgin,' Meadows said.

'How could you know that?'

I've completely blown it, Meadows thought, and whatever else I say – whatever else I feel *compelled* to say – will only make matters worse.

'Well?' Louisa demanded. 'How *do* you know?'

'Oh, come on, Louisa, it's obvious.'

'I think I'd like you to leave my house now,' Louisa said, her voice now glacier-cold.

'Yes,' Meadows agreed, standing up. 'Yes, I think that would be a good idea.'

There were four patrol cars outside the Greens' house on Balaclava Street, and their revolving lights intermittently cut through the surrounding darkness with a garish yellow beam.

There were also two ambulances, Beresford noted, as he climbed out of his car.

Two!

What the hell had gone on in there?

A young uniformed constable – they *all* looked young these days! – approached him.

'I'm sorry, sir, but there's been a serious incident here, and I'm going to have to ask you to move on,' he said.

Beresford produced his warrant card.

'Who's in charge here?' he asked.

'Well, DCI Dixon's just arrived, sir . . .'

'That's not what I asked,' Beresford snapped. 'Who's secured the crime scene?'

'That would be Inspector Flowers, sir.'

Beresford nodded. He remembered Flowers from the Danbury murder case. Monika had watched her back for her during that investigation, and it appeared – from the anonymous phone call to his flat – that Inspector Flowers was now returning the favour.

'Where's Inspector Flowers now?' he asked.

'She's with DCI Dixon, sir.'

Beresford wondered if he'd ever been this dumb when he was a uniformed constable himself, and decided it was more than possible.

'And where's DCI Dixon?' he asked. 'And don't tell me he's with Inspector Flowers.'

'They're in the kitchen,' the constable said, grinning as if Beresford had been making a joke to put him at his ease.

And maybe that's what I was doing, Beresford thought. Maybe it's a sign I'm finally maturing.

He stepped into the house, and walked down the hallway. The kitchen door was open, and he saw DCI Dixon and Inspector Flowers standing there.

Dixon's mouth dropped open when he saw him.

'What are you . . .?' he began. And then, because he was the kind of man who had both the ability and the inclination to change horses midstream, his expression switched to one of general concern, and he continued, 'This is a bad business, DI Beresford, and the press are going to crucify us unless we can find a way to keep it in hand.'

Looking over Dixon's shoulder, Beresford could see the 'bad business' he was talking about. There were two hooks set into the ceiling, which, in the old days, would have been the anchors for the clothes drying rack. Now, a thin rope – probably a clothesline – had been looped over the hooks, and hanging from the ropes – their eyes glazed, their tongues hanging out, and their feet suspended only inches from the ground – were Mr and Mrs Green.

Beresford quickly surveyed the rest of the scene. The smell of faeces in the air was enough to tell him that Mr and Mrs Green had actually died as a result of hanging, rather than being strung up when they were already dead, and if further confirmation were needed, the two three-legged foot stools, lying on their sides, provided it.

'I want you all out of here, now, chop chop!' said a voice behind him, and turning, Beresford saw Dr Shastri – resplendent, as always, in a colourful sari – standing behind him.

DCI Dixon looked resentful, but he knew you do not contradict the police doctor, especially – he thought – if she comes from a minority background, and you could be accused of being prejudiced.

'When can you give us an idea of how long they've been dead, doc?' he asked, as they passed each other on the narrow corridor.

Shastri shot him a look of dislike, then glanced up at the two corpses. 'As soon as I have inserted my little thermometer into their rectums,' she said, 'which will be when I have them back at my mortuary. But just by looking at them, I would say they have been dead for several hours.'

If that was right, then they could possibly have died while their daughter, Mary, was being cremated, Beresford thought – and he wondered if they'd planned it that way.

Out on the front step of the Greens' house, Beresford offered Inspector Flowers a cigarette, and looked down the street at the red public phone box, which was almost certainly where the call to his flat had been made from.

'Who found the bodies?' he asked Flowers.

'Their son, John,' Flowers replied. 'Apparently, he'd been out for most of the day . . .'

'I know about that. He was at his sister's cremation.'

'Oh shit, yes, he must have been. And then he came home to this. Poor little bugger.'

'Did he call us himself?'

'No, the Greens don't have a telephone.' Flowers paused. 'They don't seem to have a television, either. What kind of family is it – in this day and age – that doesn't have a television?'

'A weird one,' Beresford acknowledged. 'So what did he do when he found the bodies?'

'He went next door, and asked the neighbours to phone – I say "neighbours", but I'm only using the word in the geographical sense – they told me that none of the Green family have ever really spoken to them in the five years they've been living there.'

'Where's John now?' Beresford asked.

'He was feeling very cold, so I put him in one of patrol cars with a blanket round him. But even then, he wouldn't stop shivering, so I had him taken to Whitebridge General. I think they're planning to keep him in overnight.'

'Do you think it really was a suicide?' Beresford said.

'Do you mean, rather than a double murder which was staged to look like a suicide?'

'Exactly.'

'I think it really was suicide,' Flowers said. 'I think that, for reasons best known to themselves, they took two knotted pieces of clothes line and hanged themselves in their own kitchen. As far as timing goes, it's possible that he waited until she was dead before hanging himself, or she waited until he was dead. But my gut tells me it wasn't like that. My gut tells me they went together.'

'That's what my gut tells me, too,' Beresford said.

Inspector Flowers shuddered. 'Just imagine it,' she said. 'Just imagine hanging there – feeling the life being squeezed out of you – and watching your partner die at the same time. Why do you think they did it that way?'

'Maybe each one wanted to make sure the other didn't back

out at the last minute,' Beresford suggested. 'Or maybe if they
had to die, they wanted to die together.'

'Makes you think, doesn't it?' Flowers said.

'Yes, it does,' Beresford agreed, 'and honestly, I'd much rather
it didn't.' He finished his cigarette, snipped the glowing end off
with his thumb and forefinger nails, and put the filter in his pocket.
He glanced at the phone box again, and pictured Flowers making
the call, and one of her team telling her that she was wanted.
'Thanks for your help,' he said.

'Help?' Inspector Flowers repeated. 'Help? I have no idea what
you're talking about, DI Beresford.'

When Austen Chalmers had announced to his friends that he needed
a complete break from the office, and had decided to spend a week
hiking and rough camping on the moors, they'd rolled their eyes
in what they probably considered was a comical manner and asked
him if he was quite sure he wanted to do that.

'You're not exactly an old man,' they'd said, 'but let's face it,
Austen, you're no spring chicken either – and rough camping is
a young man's sport.'

'I may be forty-two,' he'd responded, somewhat offended, 'but
I'm as fit as I ever was.'

It wasn't true – that thing about the fitness – he very soon realized. Or perhaps it was and it was the conditions, rather than he
himself, which had changed. It was perfectly possible, he supposed,
that the ground could have become much harder than it used to be
when he was young, and that miles could have been recalibrated to
make them twice as long as he remembered. While he wasn't looking,
weights could have been changed, too, so that a twenty-pound load
was now much heavier than what had been a twenty-pound
load back in the day. But it was much more likely, he reluctantly
conceded, that his friends had been right, and hiking and rough
camping were a young man's game.

His pride made him stick it out for three days, but on the fourth,
his blisters and his aches forced him to hobble to a very pleasant
inn on the edge of the moors, where, on presentation of that basic
and essential survival tool – the credit card – he was warmly
welcomed in.

A good soak in the bath did wonders for his body, and a meal which hadn't come out of a can seemed to positively nourish his soul. He retired early, with half a bottle of whisky to keep him company, to watch television in his room until he fell asleep.

While he'd been out on the moors, there'd been a murder in one of the nearby towns, he learned from the local news. And not just a murder – a detective chief inspector had been seriously injured, as well.

A Honda 250cc motorcycle suddenly appeared on the screen, for no reason Chalmers could discern.

'The police are looking for this motorbike, which the murderer may have been riding,' said the voiceover. 'If you have any knowledge of its whereabouts, please contact the Mid Lancs police as soon as possible.'

Chalmers' mind travelled back to Monday morning, and to the lad – he could remember his face quite distinctly – rolling the bike into the lake at the bottom of the abandoned quarry. It had seemed crazy at the time, but suddenly it was making a lot of sense.

He picked up the bedside phone, and dialled the number that was still on the screen.

Beresford sat down next to Monika's bed. He'd been told by the nurse on duty that there'd be no harm in holding her hand, as long as he held it lightly, so that was what he did.

Looking down at the hands, it occurred to him that in all their years of friendship . . .

Friendship! Why was he calling it *friendship*, when he knew it was much more than that?

In all the years they had *loved* each other, they'd never been as physically intimate as this, and now they were, one of them might not even be aware of it.

'I miss you, Monika,' he said. 'I don't mean as a friend – though God knows, I miss you there – I mean as a boss. We all miss you. Without you, we're all drifting away from what we really are. Meadows is becoming the kinder face of policing – if you can believe that. Crane's slipping into Meadows's shoes, and has started to see finding a way round laid-down procedures as some kind of sport. And me? I used to think I could do your job, but I can't. I was a pretty good inspector with you in charge, but now you're not there, I feel more like a sergeant, and if it goes on for much longer, I'll be thinking like a constable again.'

'Don't beat yourself up,' said a voice from the doorway. 'You're doing the best you can in the circumstances.'

Beresford smiled gratefully at Meadows, but he was thinking that their working relationship had always been slightly prickly and confrontational, and the fact that she was changing now could only mean that she was as frightened as he was, and needed to cling to him for comfort.

'Kate's just been to see Louisa,' Beresford said to Paniatowski, 'and she's fine, isn't she, Kate?'

'Yes,' Meadows said, though her expression indicated quite the reverse. 'Of course, she misses you and she wants you home again, but she's holding up very well. She's got a lot of balls – just like her mother.'

'Loui'a,' Monika said, in a hoarse, agonized voice. 'Twin . . .'

'They're all fine,' Beresford assured her. 'The twins don't even realize anything is wrong.'

'Loui'a . . . twin . . .' Monika said again.

'You shouldn't worry,' Beresford assured her. 'If it will make you happier, I'll take the twins to the zoo tomorrow.'

'Loui'a . . . twin . . .' Monika screamed. 'Loui'a . . . twin . . .'

The medical instruments which surrounded her were going crazy.

'I'd better call a doctor,' Meadows said.

And Beresford, fighting for breath, could say nothing.

'She's settled down again now,' the doctor told Meadows and Beresford. 'Hopefully, she'll have a peaceful night.'

'What does it mean that she suddenly started speaking like that?' Beresford asked, anguished.

'I'm afraid I can't discuss Ms Paniatowski's condition with someone who is not a relative,' the doctor said.

'Oh, I think that you could – if you really forced yourself to,' Meadows said sweetly.

'When I entered this profession, I swore the Hippocratic Oath, young lady,' the doctor said severely.

'Yes, but you must admit, there's scope for interpretation, if you want there to be,' Meadows said.

She was still sounding reasonable, Beresford thought – although God alone knew how long that would last.

'The Hippocratic Oath is not open to interpretation of any kind,' the doctor said.

'Oh well, if you're going to be so legalistic about things . . .' Meadows said, and then left the rest of the sentence hanging.

'What do you mean?' the doctor asked, and he was already starting to sound uneasy.

'I mean that I suppose I had better enforce the law without allowing any scope for interpretation.'

'Quite right, too – the law is the law,' the doctor said, though he was definitely sensing danger now.

'Do you know how many times the average person breaks the law – in its most strictly enforceable sense – every day?' Meadows asked. 'Of course, we normally turn a blind eye to minor infractions, but if I'm ever to be as good a police woman as you are a doctor . . .'

'Are you threatening me,' the doctor asked, outraged.

'No,' Meadows said. 'Threatening is based on "if you don't do this, I'll do that", whereas what I am saying is, "if you *do* do this, I will prosecute you as the law demands". So if you end up spending half your time in court, answering a series of petty charges, it's really your fault, isn't it?'

'DS Meadows wouldn't normally talk to you like this, and she's only doing it now because she really does care about Monika,' Beresford said, offering the doctor a face-saving lifebelt. 'I care, too.'

'Well, since you are both so obviously concerned, I don't suppose there's any harm in giving you my opinion,' the doctor said, grabbing the lifebelt with both hands. 'What happened earlier may have been a freak occurrence, which means nothing at all in the long term. On the other hand . . .' he paused. 'How can I best explain it to laymen like yourselves? It might help if you could picture Ms Paniatowski as being in a lake, trapped under a layer of ice. What you witnessed a few minutes ago may have been the first real indication that she is ready to break that ice and burst through to the surface again.'

'May have been?' Meadows said.

'Yes.'

'What else could it have been?'

The doctor sighed. 'It could have been the last desperate tapping on the underside of the ice before she sinks forever,' he said.

FIFTEEN

Wednesday

The first patrol cars had arrived just after dawn had broken, the lorries, with the hydraulic cranes on their flatbeds, turned up about half an hour later. And still, though another hour had passed, and the sun was climbing high in the sky, nothing seemed to have been done.

'What's the delay?' DS Higgins asked the sergeant in charge of the frogman unit impatiently. 'Why aren't your lads already in the water?'

'We have to do a risk assessment first,' explained the sergeant, whose name was Jenkins.

'A bloody sodding risk assessment!' Higgins snorted with disgust. 'What are we – policemen or pansies? Give me a wetsuit and a harness, and I'll go down there myself.'

'A, you're not insured, and B, you'd get tangled up in the harness, and bloody drown in the first thirty seconds,' Sergeant Jenkins said. 'What's your hurry, anyway, old lad? Your suspect's not going anywhere, is he?'

It's not my bloody suspect I'm worried about, Higgins thought – it's Paniatowski's team.

The problem was, he didn't know what they were doing, and he couldn't trust them not to screw things up for him, either accidentally or with malice aforethought. He needed to present Rhino Dixon with a clear-cut and dried solution to the case. What he *didn't* need was for Beresford to either share the credit or put forward some other solution.

'We're ready when you are, skipper,' one of the frogmen called out to Jenkins.

'Off you go, then,' the sergeant said, 'and for God's sake be careful, because who knows what kind of shit there is down there.'

Their harnesses attached to the crane, the two frogmen walked backwards down the steep slope, their rubber feet flip-flopping as they went. Once they were immersed in the pit, they trod water while they released their harnesses, then did a backwards aquatic somersault, and disappeared from sight.

They emerged again about half a minute later.

'It goes almost straight down for about twenty feet, does this bugger,' one of them called out. 'The motorbike's at the bottom.'

'Can you get it?' Jenkins asked.

'Should be able to, unless there's some problem we've missed,' the diver said.

The lorries had had their backs to the pit, but now one of them manoeuvred into a sideways on position, so that the arm of its hydraulic crane was as far over the water as possible.

Then, slowly and carefully, a heavy chain with a large hook on the end of it was lowered down into the water.

The divers counted the number of links being submerged, and when they judged there was enough of the chain under the water to serve their purposes, they called a halt.

Higgins watched the divers submerge themselves close to the hanging chain. He realized he was silently counting to himself.

'One hundred, two hundred, three hundred . . .'

He had reached 'three thousand' when the divers emerged again, some distance from the chain.

'Haul away,' one of them called out.

The crane began to wind the chain around its capstan, and after less than a minute, the hook emerged with the red motorbike attached to it.

'Good job, lads,' Sergeant Jenkins called to his divers.

Now I've got you, you young bastard, DS Higgins thought.

Crane stood at the end of the platform on Whitebridge railway station, and watched George Oppenheimer climb ponderously down from the train.

Oppenheimer had not changed much since their days at university. He still had a roundish face, framed by unruly curly black hair; still had a body shaped like a pear, which he habitually kept encased in a series of tweed suits which had probably been made years before either he – or Crane – had been born.

He was a strange feller, Crane thought (though back in his Oxford days, he'd probably have called him a strange chap).

George Halston Oppenheimer III came from an old New York family which had so much money that, as a traditional Whitebridge saying had it, he could have paid some other feller to scratch his arse for him, if he'd been so inclined.

Yet he didn't desire luxury – or even basic comforts. His room in college was spartan, and he lived off a diet which consisted mainly of donuts, Oreo cookies and Coca-Cola (all purchased in bulk from a contact at the nearby American Air Force Base).

Apart from visits to the Bodleian Library, he rarely left his rooms, and if Crane hadn't happened to live on the same staircase, they would probably never have met.

Crane stepped into the centre of the platform, confident that if he hadn't, Oppenheimer would have walked past him. It wasn't that Oppenheimer wouldn't have recognized him if he'd been looking, he thought – it was more the case that Oppenheimer wouldn't have bothered to look.

The New Yorker cared about one thing and one thing only – the study of cults – and though he was not, strictly speaking, an *acknowledged* world expert, Crane suspected that a world expert was exactly what he was.

'Ah, Crane,' Oppenheimer said, finding his way blocked. 'I believe you have an interesting case study for me.'

'I believe I do,' Crane agreed.

Higgins stood with Andrew Selby, Hodges' solicitor, watching Barry Hodges lining up against a wall with several other men of a similar description.

'You'll have your work cut out on this one,' he said jovially, 'especially now we've found the bike.'

'Let me make one thing clear to you, sergeant,' Selby said. 'I consider my client to be a repulsive human being, and if it were the law that repulsive human beings should be vaporized, I'd have absolutely no difficulty in condemning him myself. But at the same time, I do not believe – even for a second – that he killed Mary Green.'

'Oh dear, oh dear, oh dear, Mr Selby,' Higgins said, 'you're going to end up *so* disappointed.'

The first witness – Austen Chambers, the ex-rough camper – was brought into the room.

'Now they can't see you, so you've no need to worry,' Higgins said. 'Just take your time, and don't speak until you're sure.'

'I don't need to take my time,' Chambers said. 'The man I saw throwing the motorbike into the quarry was number four.'

The second witness was the bus driver who'd been operating the Monday morning moorland bus service.

'It's number four,' he said.

'You're sure of that?'

'Positive. See, I hardly ever pick up passengers there – I'm not even sure why there's a stop there at all – and if he hadn't been running, he'd have missed the bus, so it stuck in my mind.'

Higgins beamed at Selby. 'This is going to be a *good* day for the forces of law and order,' he said.

John Green – pale but calm – looked across the interview table at Meadows and said, 'Why am I here?'

'Your sister has been murdered, and your mother and father have both died in dramatic circumstances,' Meadows said, in a kindly voice which, under different circumstances, Beresford would have found almost comical. 'You must surely have been expecting to be questioned by the police, John.'

'I suppose I must,' Green conceded, 'but isn't it a legal requirement that an adult who has nothing to do with the investigation should be present to monitor the interview?'

'We only have to do that if we're questioning a child – but you're not a child, are you?'

'I'm under eighteen. Doesn't that make me a child?'

'Are you sure you're under eighteen?'

'Yes.'

Meadows reached into the folder lying in front of her, and extracted a small brown document. She opened it, and laid it out before him.

'Do you know what this is, John?' she asked.

'It's a birth certificate. Where did you get it?'

'It was in the drawer at your house.'

'Are you allowed to do this kind of thing?' Green asked.

'Oh yes,' Meadows assured him. 'It's all been done by the book. Is this *your* birth certificate, John?'

'Yes.'

'Then it seems you turned eighteen yesterday, so legally, you're no longer a child.'

'The lab says the birth certificate is probably a forgery,' Crane told Oppenheimer, in the room on the other side of the two-way mirror. 'It's a *very good* forgery, but a forgery nonetheless.'

'We've got him over a barrel,' Beresford added. 'If he believes the birth certificate is genuine, then he also believes that he's eighteen. If, in fact, he's *under* eighteen and knows it, he daren't admit it, because that would also be admitting the forgery.'

'Fascinating,' George Oppenheimer said. 'Why would anyone watch television when they can see a show like this?'

'Maybe because most people *can't* actually see a show like this,' Crane suggested.

'Ah yes, that would explain it,' Oppenheimer said.

'I'd forgotten all about the birthday,' John Green told Meadows.

'*The* birthday?' Meadows repeated. 'Why did you say that, and not *my* birthday?'

'I don't know.'

'It's perfectly understandable, given what you've been through, that you would forget your birthday,' Meadows said.

'I probably wouldn't have remembered under any other circumstances, either,' John Green said. 'We don't really set much store by birthdays in my family.'

'In much the same way as you don't set much store by Christmas and Easter?' Meadows asked.

'That's right.'

'Even though, despite what you told me the last time we talked, you're Christians.'

'Who told you that?' Green demanded. And then his face relaxed. 'Of course, it was Louisa.'

'Before we go any further, I want to make sure you're thoroughly aware of your rights,' Meadows said. 'Even though you've not been charged with anything, you're entitled to have a lawyer present. If you want one, and if you can't afford to pay, one will be provided free of charge.'

'I don't want a lawyer,' Green said.

'Are you sure of that?'

'Yes.'

'Absolutely sure?'

'Yes.'

'If he *is* a cult member, as you suspect, then the last thing he will want is a lawyer getting involved,' Oppenheimer said.

'But surely, if he wants to stop us probing into the cult, having a lawyer with him would be a great help,' Beresford said.

'It would be a bit like a goat that was afraid of being eaten by a lion calling in a tiger to help it out,' Oppenheimer said. 'The integrity of the cult is of paramount importance. A lawyer – asking questions, poking around – is a cure which is as bad as the disease.' He unwrapped an Oreo and raised it to his mouth. 'Of course,' he said, before enveloping the cookie in his fat lips, 'it may just be the case that he doesn't like lawyers. I don't care for them myself – but perhaps that's because three of my uncles are lawyers.'

'Do you have any idea why your parents might have committed suicide?' Meadows asked.

'Perhaps they found the thought of living on without Mary unbearable,' John Green suggested. 'Perhaps her death was no more than the straw that finally broke the poor camel's back – the final proof that the world is an intolerable place in which to exist.'

'Was it because they found it such an intolerable place that your father didn't have a job?' Meadows asked.

'He did have a job.'

'Oh! What job would that be?'

'I don't know, exactly.'

'Come on, now,' Meadows said, 'you're an intelligent, curious, young man. You must, at some point, have asked your father what he did for a living. That would be only natural.'

'It may seem natural to you, but it simply didn't occur to me.'

'We both know he didn't have a job,' Meadows said. 'Certainly, he left home every morning wearing a boiler suit, but we can find no record of him working anywhere.'

'Maybe he was just part of the black economy that I keep reading about in the broadsheet newspapers,' John Green suggested.

'He's a cocky young bastard, isn't he?' Beresford said. 'I've never seen a kid of his age act so confidently under interrogation – and I'm including in that the ones who already have a criminal record, know the drill, and really don't give a shit about what happens to them next.'

'He reminds me of Martin Luther,' Crane said reflectively.

'Black vicar, led a lot of marches, got himself shot,' Beresford said. 'Is that who you're talking about?'

'No, not Martin Luther King, just Martin Luther, the man he was named after.'

'Was he American, too?'

'No, he was German – a professor at Wittenberg University.'

'And when would this have been?'

'Roughly four hundred years ago.'

'That would be a bit before my time, then,' Beresford said.

Crane smiled. 'That's right, sir.'

'So what was so special about him?'

'Luther was one of the first men to challenge the Catholic Church, and he was called before the parliament in Worms – which was presided over by the big man of Europe, the Holy Roman Emperor – to explain himself. Of course, what everybody else meant by the term "explaining himself" was issuing a grovelling apology and begging for forgiveness. But it didn't happen that way. Luther was terrified of appearing before the emperor – his stomach was so upset he was almost permanently on the bog – but he was sure he was right in what he thought, and he knew there was an invisible army of supporters standing behind him, who thought just like he did. And that's what this lad's got, if you ask me – an invisible army of supporters standing behind him.'

'Maybe,' Beresford conceded, slightly dubiously, 'but maybe it's nothing to do with belonging to a cult – maybe he's just a cocky little shit.'

'Come to think of it, John, your family isn't really that unusual,' Meadows said musingly. 'Several of the pupils who attended your school seem to have had fathers who pretended to work, but didn't.'

'I don't know anything about that.'.

'And all those families have mysteriously disappeared.'

'I don't know about that, either.'

'Why don't you tell me about Mrs Brown?' Meadows suggested.

'I never met Mrs Brown.'

'You never met her – even though your sister Mary spent every weekend with her?'

'That's right.'

'How did Mary meet her?'

'I don't know.'

'Didn't she tell you?'

'I was very fond of my sister, but we didn't spend a great deal of time talking about what each of us was doing.'

George Oppenheimer had been getting more and more interested as the interrogation progressed, but now the look which came to his face was like that of a child who – unexpectedly and against all odds – had been told that it's Christmas Day, and will be all week!

'This is truly fascinating,' he told Crane and Beresford. 'I wasn't ever sure that they even existed any more, and I certainly never suspected – not for a moment – that there were any of them over here in England.'

'Any of who?' Crane asked.

Oppenheimer looked at him blankly, as if unable to understand why one of the smartest people he had met at university should even need to ask so obvious a question.

'Who?' he said. 'Why, the Hidden, of course.'

'I've never heard of them,' Crane confessed. 'What do they do? What do they believe?'

But Oppenheimer wasn't really listening.

'Do you want to give Sergeant Meadows a question that I think will break through his protective shell?' he asked Beresford.

'Definitely.'

'And can I talk to Sergeant Meadows directly, through that microphone?'

'Yes.'

Oppenheimer leant over the microphone, and pressed the button.

'Tell John Green that though you're sure he'll never admit to it, you know with absolute certainty that he's a Trusted One,' he said.

'How long have you been a Trusted One?' Meadows asked John Green.

Green had been slouching forward – elbows on the table – but now he was suddenly sitting bolt upright.

'I have absolutely no idea what it is you're talking about,' he said, unconvincingly.

'I know you *are* a Trusted One, so there's no point in denying it,' Meadows said harshly.

'As I've just said, I really have no idea—'

'Are you ashamed of it?'

'—what you're referring to.'

'Well, from looking at you, I'd guess you don't need many qualifications to be offered the job, or it would have gone to someone else. It's probably one of those jobs that nobody wants anyway, and only the poor in spirit, or the stupid, can be persuaded to take it on.'

'It's not like . . .'

'What was that you started to say?'

'Nothing.'

'How long have you held this position that only a fool would occupy? A year? Two years?'

'You have no idea – no idea at all – what you must endure once you've been chosen to be a Trusted One!' John Green said angrily.

On the other side of the plate glass, his cheeks bulging and the light flashing off his thick glasses, George Oppenheimer punched the air with delight.

'As it is written in the Dead Sea Scrolls and many other sacred texts – bingo!' he said.

SIXTEEN

Sergeant Higgins lent back in his chair like a man who, if he was wearing a hat, would have tipped it at a jaunty angle.

'Well, well, Barry boy, I told you we'd get the evidence we needed – and we have,' he said.

'I've no idea what you're talking about,' Barry Hodges replied sullenly.

'Your bike, lad,' Higgins said, sliding a glossy picture of the recovered Honda across the table.

'It's not my bike,' Hodges said.

'It matches the description half a dozen people have given of your bike. And even more telling, it has your fingerprints all over it,' Higgins said. 'If that doesn't make it your bike, then I don't know what does.'

'You're just bluffing,' Hodges said. 'It can't have my fingerprints on it, because . . .'

'Because what?'

'Nothing.'

'Because it's been at the bottom of a quarry pit for the last three days? Is that what you were going to say?'

'Yes,' Hodges said instinctively, then a look of horrified realization came to his face, and he shook his head violently. 'I mean *no*.'

'No, that wasn't what you were going to say? Or no, you didn't throw your bike into the quarry.'

'I meant it wasn't what I was going to say, because I didn't know *where* the bike was.'

'Your bike?'

'The bike in the picture.'

'I've got two reliable eye witnesses who'll swear that you did throw it in,' Higgins said, 'but that's beside the point, isn't it, because what we should really be talking about is the fingerprints. You seem to think that after three days underwater, all the fingerprints will have been destroyed, don't you? Well, you're quite wrong about that, my old son. Fingerprints can survive under water for at least five days, and if you don't believe me – if you think I'm trying to trick you – why don't you ask your solicitor?'

Hodges turned to Selby, and Selby nodded that yes, that was true.

'And guess who else's fingerprints we found on that bike of yours, Barry,' Higgins said. 'We found Mary Green's.'

After a short, whispered conversation with his solicitor, Hodges said, 'All right, I did know her.'

'How well?'

'We went out together a few times.'

'Where did you meet her?'

'At the supermarket where I work. Most of the time, I'm stuck in the warehouse, but now and again, when they're very busy, they bring me out to stack shelves. That's what I was doing when I met Mary – stacking shelves.'

'And what happened?'

'I asked her out for a coffee, and she said yes.'

'What attracted you to her?'

'Well, she was a good-looking girl, wasn't she, and she seemed the sort of girl who, if you treated her right would . . . you know . . .'

'No,' Higgins said. 'I don't know.'

'You must.'

'Maybe I do, and maybe I don't,' Higgins said, 'but I'd appreciate it if you'd spell it out for me.'

'She looked like the kind of girl who, if you treated her right, would be very nice to you in return. Is that clear enough for you?'

'It'll do for the present,' Higgins conceded. 'So you started seeing each other regularly, did you?'

'Nearly every Sunday.'

'Where did you go?'

'Mostly into the country.'

'Did you introduce her to any of your friends?'

'No.'

'Why was that?'

'She didn't want me to.'

'You seem to have let her push you around a lot,' Higgins said. 'Just what kind of man are you?'

Despite the situation he found himself in, Hodges smirked. 'I always let them have their own way – until they give me what I want.'

'Fancy yourself as a bit of a Casanova, do you?' Higgins asked.

'You what? I don't know what you're talking about?'

'You think you're pretty hot at pulling girls?'

'There's no *think* about it,' Hodges said.

Yes, I can see it, Higgins thought. To me he might seem a snivelling little shit whose face I'd take the greatest pleasure in rearranging, but a lot of young girls might well find him attractive.

'So you pretty much let the girls have their own way until they give you what you want. Isn't that what you said?' he asked.

'That's right.'

'And did Mary give you what you wanted?'

'No.'

'No, she didn't, did she? We know you didn't get what you wanted, because she died a virgin. Was it when she told you she wasn't going to spread her legs for you that you lost your temper and killed her!'

'No,' Hodges said, 'I didn't kill her. Apart from her pressing up against me on the bike, and the odd necking session, I never even touched her.'

'Tell me what happened that day, then,' Higgins suggested.

'We went to the hall. It cost eight pounds to get in, and I paid it all, because she never had any money. We went to the woods.' Barry paused. 'There's something I should tell you about what had happened before.'

'Go on.'

'The Sunday before last Sunday, I'd told her that I was going to break up with her.'

'Because she'd been taking too long to start being nice to you?'

'Yes.'

'So what happened?'

'She cried a bit, then she said if that was really what I wanted, she'd go along with it the next Sunday.'

'That's last Sunday, the Sunday on which she died, that we're talking about now?'

'Yes.'

'So when you went into the woods last Sunday, you really thought you were about to get your end away?'

'Yes.'

'And what actually happened?'

'She said she'd been talking it through with this man – a trustee, I think she said he was . . .'

'A trustee of what?'

'I don't know. She didn't explain. I think he was the feller who the family went to for advice.'

'And what did this trustee say?'

'He told her she couldn't do it with me.'

'So what happened then?'

'I said that if that was how things were, she could bloody well find her own way home.'

'You said it all quite calmly?'

'Yes.'

'You didn't lose your temper at any point?'

'No. Why would I? So what if she wouldn't come across. There are plenty of other fish in the sea.'

'I see,' Higgins said. 'Well, thank you for explaining that to me. Would you mind if I asked one personal question, just for my own satisfaction?'

'Err . . . yes,' Hodges said cautiously.

'I can understand you strangling her . . .'

'I didn't . . .'

'Just let me finish, lad. I can understand you strangling her – in my opinion, there was plenty of provocation, and I might have done the same in your shoes – but what I don't understand is why, after that, you should flush out her vagina with hot tea.'

'What?' Hodges asked, his complexion turning a light shade of green.

'I don't see why you should want to give her pussy a scalding hot PG Tips shampoo,' Higgins said calmly.

Hodges rose shakily to his feet, and staggered towards the door. He was only halfway there when his body suddenly jack-knifed, and he was violently sick all over the floor.

The solicitor looked at DS Higgins over the top of his half-moon glasses.

'Either my client is the greatest actor since the young Olivier first trod the boards,' he drawled, 'or what you've just said is complete news to him.'

George Oppenheimer looked cautiously around the public bar of the Drum and Monkey.

'Do you guys really use this place?' he asked, dubiously, as if he thought this was no more than an elaborate practical joke.

'Yes, we use it all the time,' Beresford assured him.

'What would you like to drink, George?' Crane asked.

'A sarsaparilla would be good,' Oppenheimer said.

'In the Drum, a sarsaparilla would be more than good – it would be a bloody miracle,' Beresford said. 'Would you settle for a glass of lemonade?'

'I guess,' Oppenheimer said, though he did not sound totally convinced of the wisdom of agreeing.

'So tell us about the Hidden,' Colin Beresford said, once the drinks had arrived.

'Sure,' Oppenheimer agreed, 'but first I have to put things into context.' He took a sip of his lemonade, and pulled a face. 'It's kinda like 7UP, but only *kinda*, if you know what I mean,' he said to Crane, as if he had come to regard the detective constable as his protector in the hostile universe which seemed to exist beyond the bounds of Oxford. 'Are you sure it's all right to drink it?'

'It's all right,' Crane said.

'OK,' Oppenheimer said. 'I assume that you're all familiar with the Book of Job?'

'I am,' Crane said.

'I thought you were an atheist, Jack,' Kate Meadows said, her amusement obvious. 'Or do you just say you are because you think it gives you a certain intellectual air?'

'I am an atheist,' Crane said, 'but once, in the golden days before I immersed myself in this sewer we affectionately call the Mid Lancs police force, I was also a student of literature. And that is what the Book of Job is – great literature which is used to convey great nonsense.'

'So, since we all know everything there is to know about the book—' Oppenheimer said.

'We don't,' Beresford interrupted him. 'Sergeant Meadows and I know sod all about it.'

'Really?' Oppenheimer asked.

'Really,' Beresford confirmed.

'OK, so the Book of Job opens with Job himself. Believe me, the guy has got it made – he's got a fine strong family, and is as rich as Rockefeller.' He paused. 'That's an American millionaire.'

'We know who Rockefeller is,' Beresford said.

'And yet you don't know the Book of Job,' Oppenheimer mused. 'How weird is that?' He took another sip of his lemonade. He seemed to be getting used to it. 'Anyway, the scene shifts, and we're on God's front porch up in heaven, where God is talking to Satan. "He's got a pretty high opinion of me, this guy Job, don't you think?" God says. "Oh sure, give a guy everything he wants, and he'll be real pious when he's talking about his god," Satan says. "Drop him in the shit, and it'll be quite a different matter".' He paused. 'I'm deliberately using the modern parlance to make it easier for you to follow.'

'We appreciate that, and we're very grateful,' Meadows said.

'I just don't see how it fits in with these Hidden people of yours,' Beresford said.

'You will, if you're patient,' Oppenheimer promised him. 'Now, where was I?'

'God and Satan are on God's front porch,' Crane prompted.

'Oh, yeah. They agree to carry out what you might call a social experiment. God gives Satan permission to kill Job's kids, strip him of his wealth and cover him with boils. Job does lose his faith for a while, but then he gets it back stronger than ever, and everything that's been taken from him is restored. Job's happy because he's got it all back, God's happy because he's won his bet, and the only one who's really pissed off is Satan.'

'The Hidden?' Beresford prodded.

'Their story is in some ways the same as Job's, but in some ways very different,' Oppenheimer said. 'It begins with another dialogue between God and Satan. God says that His people love Him, and Satan says, sure they do, because you're all-powerful, and who wants to cross someone who's all-powerful. But give up the power yourself – and let them have it instead – and it's a whole different story. "You want me to make them gods?" God asks. "Are you some kind of crazy man?" "No," Satan says, "I don't want you to make them gods, I just want you to give them the power to stop *you* from being God, if that's what they want to do".'

'This is getting stranger and stranger,' Meadows said.

'It's no stranger than believing that a wafer can be turned into the body of Christ,' Oppenheimer said mildly. 'Anyway, the Hidden see themselves as people with that power. And the source of that power is that when there are enough of them in one small geographical area – say, a few city blocks – the inner light of purity which each of them has combines with the light of all the others to make a beacon bright enough to lead God to earth.'

'God couldn't get here without the light?' Beresford asked.

'Indeed, that's the whole point – that's the way in which, after

His discussion with the devil, God handed the power over to them. But it's maintaining that hidden light – that purity – which is the problem.'

'I'm beginning to see how this explains their behaviour,' Crane said, excitedly.

'That must be your university education, then, because I'm still completely in the dark,' Beresford said, dourly.

'The Hidden are not allowed to live anywhere isolated, like a commune in backwoods Oregon,' Oppenheimer said, 'because it would be too easy for Satan's agents to locate them there.'

'And Satan's agents are looking for them?'

'Of course! They are constantly searching them out, because if they can destroy the inner light, they leave God totally powerless. And in order to avoid detection, the bearers of the light have chosen to be hidden in plain sight – but there's one big drawback to that.'

'How many of them are there in total?' Beresford interrupted.

Meadows rolled her eyes, as if to say, 'There goes Shagger, off at a tangent again.'

'I have absolutely no idea how many of them there are out there,' Oppenheimer said. 'Until I heard what John Green had to say, I didn't know if they even still existed.'

DS Higgins checked over both shoulders, then broke the police seal on the Greens' front door, opened the door, and stepped quickly inside.

If, later, someone involved in the investigation raised the issue of the broken seal, he could always suggest it was the work of vandals, he thought.

In fact, if anybody on the street had seen him entering the house, and reported him, he could actually use the broken seal as an alibi.

'What business had you entering the house, DS Higgins?'

'I was walking past when I noticed the seal was broken, sir, and it occurred to me that someone – maybe even the person who killed Mary Green – might be inside.'

Ignoring the ground floor, he went straight up the stairs, slipping on gloves as he did so. Three bedrooms led off the tiny landing. It should have been easy to work out which one was Mary's bedroom, because most girls – especially most *seventeen-year-old* girls – stamped their emerging personalities on their rooms with a determination which bordered on adolescent hysteria.

But it wasn't like that here – all three bedrooms were decorated and furnished in the same bland manner as the rest of the house, and it was not until he had checked the dressing table drawers in the middle one that he was sure that was where Mary had slept.

Two minutes later, he was back on the street, walking briskly away from the crime scene.

Well, that was phase one completed successfully, he told himself. Now it was time for phase two.

'Virtually everything we ever learned about the Hidden is a result of a civil suit, filed in Philadelphia at the end of the last century,' George Oppenheimer said. 'The guy who founded the Hidden was a robber baron called William McGregor, who'd made a fortune in steel and railways, you see. When he died, he left most of his money to the Hidden. His family contested the will, and it went to court, and, of course, all the details of its beliefs came out during cross examination.'

'How did the court rule?' Crane asked.

'It ruled in favour of the Hidden,' Oppenheimer said. 'Anyway, as I was saying earlier . . .'

'Before you were so rudely interrupted by our esteemed leader,' Meadows said – *almost* under her breath.

'. . . there's one big drawback to being hidden in plain sight.'

'And what's that?' Beresford wondered.

'For their combined inner lights to shine brightly enough on what I like to think of as God's landing strip, they have to be very virtuous,' George Oppenheimer said, 'but it is hard to maintain your virtue when you are surrounded by so much corruption.'

'So while they're in society in a physical sense, they try not to be affected by it in any emotional or spiritual sense,' Crane said.

'Exactly! The children go to school, because if they didn't, it would attract the interest of the authorities – and hence the ever vigilant interest of Satan's angels. But they are instructed to learn just enough to get by. If you like, it's a bit like taking a slow poison – restrict your intake, and you'll probably survive, swallow too much and you're dead.'

'But the adults aren't in danger of being poisoned at work –
because they *don't* work!' Beresford said.

'Just so! They didn't work in William McGregor's time, and
from what you've discovered, DS Meadows, it would seem that
they still don't. Of course, in the interest of not arousing suspicion, they *pretend* that they work.'

Meadows remembered Mr Green's boiler suit, which, unlike
most boiler suits, didn't have a company logo.

'But how can they get by if they don't work?' she asked.
'Everybody needs money.'

'The Hidden will have plenty of money,' Oppenheimer told
her. 'McGregor left them millions, and that must have grown
into billions by now. I don't know how the trust in Philadelphia
gets the money to them, but you can be certain that there'll be
a way.'

'Why did Roger Smith have a television set in his front room?'
Meadows asked, out of the blue.

'What do you mean?' Oppenheimer asked.

'The Greens and Mrs Brown didn't have television sets. I assume
that's to isolate them from the outside world?'

'Yes, it probably is. There were no televisions in William
McGregor's time, so, of course, there were no rules against them,
but members of the Hidden were not allowed to read newspapers
or magazines, nor go to the theatre, which is pretty much the same
thing.'

'So why did Roger Smith have a television set in his front
room?' Meadows repeated.

'That's probably because he's one of the Trusted Ones.'

'You've used that term before. Would you like to explain what
it means?' Crane asked.

'The Hidden try to isolate themselves from the outside world
as much as possible, but they must have some dealings with it – or
rather, *some* of them must have *some* dealings with it. The ones
who do this are called the Trusted Ones, because they are the
strong ones – the ones who can be trusted to immerse themselves
in the corruption without it polluting them. In fact, it's not only
their job to come into contact with the outside world – they also
have to understand it, so they can predict how it will react, and
thus know how to guide their people.'

'And in order to understand the world as it is, it's necessary for them to watch television,' Meadows said.

'Exactly. It's a job of the Trusted Ones to get the Hidden to act as if they were normal, without, of course, them actually *being* normal.'

But because the Trusted Ones weren't fully part of the real world either, they didn't get it quite right, thought Meadows, picturing the front parlours which looked more like film sets than rooms in normal houses.

'To sum up, I wouldn't exactly call the Trusted Ones robot masters – but they come pretty damn close to it,' Oppenheimer said.

Meadows remembered breaking the news of Mary Green's death to her parents, and how they had seemed totally incapable of dealing with it. But was that surprising, when they had been trained to take no decisions of their own?

'John Green told me he wasn't a Trusted One,' she said to Oppenheimer. 'Was he lying to me?'

'No, it was stupid of me even to suggest that he was – though it seems to have worked out well in the end,' Oppenheimer said. 'What I'd forgotten, you see, is that you can't be a Trusted One until you turn twenty-one. But though he doesn't hold that post, I have absolutely no doubt that he was training for it.'

And that was where all his confidence came from, Meadows thought. In a way, it was understandable – if you were plucked from the crowd and told by everyone that you were special, it was hard not to start to believe it yourself.

'If I remember rightly, you told me that he and two other boys were playing some kind of game with Roger Smith the day Mary Green was killed,' Oppenheimer said. 'That was almost certainly a way of camouflaging a training session.'

'Let's cut to the chase,' said Beresford, who had decided there'd been far too much airy-fairy discussion. 'It doesn't sound to me like the kind of cult that would practice ritual sacrifice. Is that right?'

'Anything's possible,' Oppenheimer said. 'It's eighty years since we've had a clear picture of them, and in that time, a lot of things could have changed. But given their founding rules and principles, I doubt the Hidden would ever have got to the point where they considered the spilling of blood in a ritualistic way to be a good thing.'

'Whoever killed Mary Green washed her vagina out with tea,' Beresford said. 'Could that be part of a ritual?'

'If it is, it's not a ritual I've heard of. In fact, the Hidden don't really have rituals, because rituals tend to be practiced when a group is gathered together – and *their* whole point, because they *are* the Hidden, is to have as little *direct* contact with each other as possible.'

'But they wouldn't have liked Mary Green seeing someone who wasn't a member of the group, would they?'

'It's a tad stronger than "wouldn't like",' Oppenheimer said. 'They would have seen it as a definite threat to their survival – and that means, of course, to *God's* survival.'

SEVENTEEN

Mrs Hodges was not exactly feeling in the greatest of spirits anyway, but her heart sank even further when she opened her front door and saw the two detectives standing there.

'You again!' she said. 'When will it ever end?'

'It will end when either we're satisfied, or the magistrate refuses to renew our search warrant,' DS Higgins told her. 'And now, madam, I'd be grateful if you'd go into the kitchen while we carry out our search.'

'But you've already searched the whole house from top to bottom twice,' Mrs Hodges protested.

'Then this will be the third time, won't it?' Higgins said. 'The kitchen – if you don't mind.'

Once she'd gone, Higgins said, 'You check the front parlour and I'll go through Barry's room.'

'And what are we looking for, exactly, skipper?' DC Bell asked.

'We're looking for anything that will link that little shit-bag Barry Hodges to the victim.'

'Like what?'

'Well, that's just it, DC Bell – until we find it, we won't know, will we?' Higgins asked.

He went upstairs, to Barry Hodges' bedroom, and looked around him.

'Now where would young Barry hide things he didn't want his nosy bloody mother to see?' he asked himself aloud.

He found his answer in the wardrobe, in the form of a cardboard box. Inside the box were harmless-looking motorbike magazines, but underneath them there were other magazines, which could not be bought in ordinary shops, containing photographs of people doing things that were beyond a lot of folks' imagination and bodily flexibility.

'Well, you are a dirty little bastard, aren't you, Barry,' he said, with considerable satisfaction.

Two minutes later he went downstairs to the parlour, where Bell was trying to look both busy and conscientious.

'Come upstairs, Ding-dong,' he said. 'You search the room, and I'll watch you. It'll be a sort of training exercise.'

It took Bell five minutes to find the cardboard box in the wardrobe, and when he did, he merely took the lid off, looked at the top motorcycling magazine, and put the lid in place again.

'Hang on,' Higgins said, 'aren't you going to look inside?'

'It will have been searched twice before, skip,' Bell said.

'Yes, and there's just a chance that the fellers who did it were bungling idiots who didn't recognize a clue when it was staring them in the face,' Higgins said. 'Open the box again, lad.'

When Bell found the magazines at the bottom of the box, his eyes positively bulged.

'These look like they might be a bit spicy, skip,' he said.

'Pick one up,' Higgins suggested. 'Give it a shake to see if there's a free gift inside.'

Bell did as he'd been instructed, and a pair of panties, which had been nestling in the middle, fell onto the bedroom floor.

'Well, well, well,' Higgins said. 'I wonder who they belong to.'

Meadows smiled at John Green across the table in Interview Room B.

'Earlier this morning, when I asked you if you knew why your mother and father hanged themselves, you said that you thought it was because they couldn't face the world. But I don't think that *is* what you really thought. I think you lied in an attempt to protect your secret, but that secret's out now – now we know all about the Hidden – so there's no point in lying any more, is there?'

'No,' John Green said. 'I don't suppose there is.'

'So why *do* you think they killed themselves?'

'I think that they were afraid that they would not be strong enough to keep a secret under pressure from all your questioning.'

'And what secret might that be?'

'Where the Hidden have gone.'

'They would have known that?'

'Yes, they stayed behind to give the others a chance to escape, but they will have been told where to find them once this is all over.'

'Do *you* know where the Hidden have gone?' Meadows asked.

'No.'

'Are you sure about that?'

'I have been being trained to become a Trusted One since I was selected at the age of nine,' John Green said, 'but until I reach twenty-one, I am a child, and children are not told where we will hide from the devil next.'

'Will they come back for you?'

'No. I don't think I have betrayed them, but they will not see it that way. Besides, they know the devil's dark angels will be watching me, and it is too much of a risk.'

'So what happens next?' Meadows asked.

'I will have to live a normal life – there is no choice in the matter.' John Green smiled. It was a poignant smile. 'It feels as if a great weight has been lifted off my shoulders.'

'Can I ask you about last Sunday?' Meadows asked.

'I suppose so.'

'Were you, Philip Jones and Michael Gray at Roger Smith's house all day?'

'Yes.'

'But not to play Diplomacy?'

'No, not to play Diplomacy. Roger is a Trusted One, and he was training us in our duties.'

'And you *were* there all day?'

'Yes.'

'*All* of you?'

'Yes.'

'You're lying, John.'

'Roger Smith was away for some time,' Green admitted.

'How much time?'

'Three or four hours.'

'In the evening?'

'In the afternoon.'

'Does he have a car?'

'No, he doesn't even know how to drive. None of us do. Driving leads to meeting lots of new people, and meeting lots of new people leads to corruption and the weakening of the light.'

'Why didn't you tell us before that Smith had been away for most of the afternoon?'

'Roger asked me not to.'

'Do you know why?'

'It is not for me to question a Trusted One.'

'So why are you telling me now?'

'Whatever the reason he did not wish you to know where he was, it doesn't matter now, because he is gone and you will never find him.'

'Hasn't it occurred to you that Smith was missing just at the time your sister was killed?' Meadows asked.

'He would not have killed Mary.'

'How can you be so sure?'

'He is a Trusted One. He had a duty to protect her.'

'But didn't he have a duty to protect the group as a whole?'

'Of course he did.'

'And by her actions, wasn't Mary threatening the safety of the group?'

John Green suddenly put his hands to his face. 'Oh no,' he moaned. 'Oh God, no!'

'Guess what we found in your wardrobe, Barry?' DS Higgins said, holding up a transparent evidence envelope containing a pornographic magazine. 'You really are a dirty little wanker, aren't you?'

'I'd be grateful if you'd refrain from aiming personal abuse at my client,' Barry Hodges' solicitor said.

'Sorry, I'll re-phrase it,' Higgins said. 'You really are a dirty little masturbator, aren't you, Barry?'

'That's quite enough,' the solicitor said.

'And guess what we found inside your dirty magazine,' Higgins said. He held up a second envelope. 'These!'

'I've never seen them before,' Barry Hodges protested.

'Well, they didn't get there on their own, did they?' Higgins asked. 'Are you suggesting your mother put them there?'

'You put them there,' Hodges accused.

'No, we didn't, we *found* them there,' Higgins corrected him. 'Now the thing is, Barry, we've come to what you might call a crunch point. I'm betting these knickers belonged to Mary Green, and that we can *prove* they belonged to her. And if they are and we can, we'll be charging you with murder. But maybe I'm wrong about the knickers. Maybe they're not Mary's, or I can't prove they are – and I don't want to lose you just because of that. So here's the deal – admit to it now, and I'll see you're charged with manslaughter, and with bit of luck, you'll be out in six years. Make me chase up some more evidence and we'll go for a maximum sentence. What do you think?'

As John Green stepped through the front door of Whitebridge police headquarters, he saw the girl standing on the other side of the road.

He walked over to her and said, 'What are you doing here?'

'Waiting,' Louisa said.

'Who for?'

'For you.'

'Have you been waiting long?' he asked.

'No,' she replied, unconvincingly. 'What's been happening to you?'

'They've questioned me, and now I'm free to go.'

'So you'll be leaving Whitebridge?' she said, the disappointment evident in her voice.

'No,' he told her.

'But I thought you said . . .'

'That was before, but circumstances change. I'm planning to stay here now. I really have nowhere else to go.'

'But that's wonderful news!' Louisa said. 'I don't mean that it's wonderful news that you have nowhere else to go, I mean . . .'

'I know what you mean.'

'So where are you going to go now? Back to your house?'

'No, I can't do that, because it's still part of the investigation.'

'But they can't just throw you out on the street, with no roof over your head and only the clothes that you're wearing,' Louisa said, with a growing sense of outrage.

John smiled.

'What's so funny?' Louisa demanded.

'That you're getting so angry on my behalf – and it's not so much funny as it is touching.' The smile was still in place. 'It's not quite as bad as you imagine. They've arranged for one of the local charities to kit me out with two or three outfits, and I've got a voucher in my pocket for overnight accommodation at a hostel. They've given me some money, too, so I can buy little things like a toothbrush and toothpaste. And if I start to feel peckish – well, they tell me that Whitebridge is the pie shop capital of the universe.'

'I hate the thought of you sleeping in a hostel,' Louisa said.

'It won't be for long, and once the police have finished with it, I can move back into my own house.'

'And will you be able to do that, after all that's happened there?'

'I expect I'll get used to it.'

'You could stay at my house,' Louisa said.

'No, really, I couldn't.'

'Why not? I've got the space, and since you're not planning to leave anymore . . .'

'If we were sleeping under the same roof, it could lead to things,' he said. 'You know what I'm talking about, don't you?'

'Yes, I know,' Louisa said.

'I'm not saying it would happen, but it might,' John said.

'And what if it did happen?' Louisa asked. 'Would that be such a terrible thing? Try it for one night, rather than going to the horrible hostel. What have you got to lose?'

'I'll pick up the clothes from the charity, do the shopping I need to do, and then ring you,' he said.

'Does that mean you are willing to give it a try?' she asked.

'Yes, it does,' he replied.

Colin Beresford squared his shoulders resolutely, and knocked on DCI Dixon's office door.

'Enter,' said a gruff voice from inside, which could only have belonged to Rhino.

Dixon was sitting at his desk, ostensibly reading a report.

He looked up.

'Yes, DI Beresford?'

'We think we've got a strong line to follow on the Mary Green murder, sir,' Beresford said. 'One of this hidden cult that we've uncovered, a man called Roger Smith . . .'

'Whatever you've found out about this alleged cult doesn't really matter anymore – because we've made an arrest,' DCI Dixon said.

'Barry Hodges – the motorcyclist?' Beresford asked.

'That's right, Barry Hodges.'

'But surely, if he'd done it, his fingerprints would be on the picnic hamper,' Beresford said.

'It would have been nice if they had been,' Dixon said, sidestepping the question. 'It's always nice when convenient evidence just drops into our laps, but when it doesn't, we make do without it. And maybe Barry Hodges' fingerprints are there – maybe they're the ones that are blurred.'

'And the reason they're blurred is because there are other fingerprints – which I'm almost certain are Roger Smith's – on top of them.'

'The second set of prints were made by someone *prior* to the hamper being taken to the woods,' Dixon said, authoritatively.

'How do you know?'

'It's my job to know.'

'How could Barry Hodges have handled the hamper without getting his prints all over it?' Beresford asked.

'Look at the video,' Dixon told him. 'He was wearing leather motorcycle gauntlets.'

'He was wearing them while he was driving the bike,' Beresford said, 'but would he *still* be wearing them in the woods, on a warm summer's day?'

'You've really not thought this through, lad,' Dixon said. 'When they get to the woods, it's Mary who unstraps the basket, because she's playing the role of the little woman. That's how her prints get on it. And once he's killed her, he puts his gauntlets on *before* he picks up the basket.'

'Why would Barry hide the basket in the woods?' Beresford

asked. 'It came from his home, and he must have known it could probably be traced back to him – so why didn't he simply strap it back on his bike, and take it away?'

'He may have panicked,' Dixon said.

'He panicked so much that he spent several minutes searching out a good hiding place?' Beresford wondered.

'Look, lad, out of consideration for the fact that your team put us onto Barry Hodges in the first place, I've already given you more time – and explanation – than you're entitled to. But if I was you, I really wouldn't push it.'

'The killer didn't take it with him because he knew that a man on his own – on foot and carrying a picnic basket – would have stuck out like a sore thumb,' Beresford said.

'Barry Hodges has confessed,' Dixon said. 'He did it! What more do you want – a re-enactment of the crime by the Mid Lancs Police Amateur Dramatics Society?'

He's giving me a chance to share a joke with him, and then it will be all over, Beresford thought.

'As the officer in charge of the investigation, I'd like you to authorize a nationwide search for Roger Smith, sir,' he said.

'For Christ's sake!' Dixon exploded. 'Do you know how much that would cost?'

'We're not talking money here,' Beresford said. 'We're talking justice for Monika Paniatowski.'

'No, you're talking "DCI Dixon doesn't know his bloody arse from his bloody elbow",' Dixon said. 'I've got the right man, and I'm not going to send out any signals that there's any doubt about that.'

'If you won't do what I think needs to be done, sir, I'll have to go over your head to the chief constable,' Beresford said.

'If you do that, laddie, your career in the Mid Lancs force will be over,' Dixon growled.

'I know it will be,' Beresford said sadly. 'But I'm going to have to do it anyway.'

What was happening at the table in the public bar of the Drum and Monkey could, strictly speaking, have been called a wake, though it was nowhere near as cheerful as most wakes can be. None of the three participants had said anything to each other for quite a while, but instead were making their own mental tours of the past and mourning the end of an era.

'What did the chief constable actually tell you, sir?' Crane asked, breaking the silence.

'He said he'd had the evidence presented to him – including the signed confession – and he's satisfied that Barry Hodges killed Mary Green,' Beresford said. 'He told me I should be congratulating DCI Dixon's team – and especially DS Higgins – for exemplary police work. He went on to say that the Mid Lancs police did not encourage sore losers, and that if I wished to see my career advance, I should adopt a better attitude pretty damn quick.'

'It doesn't matter what attitude you adopt, or how quickly you adopt it,' Meadows said. 'Dixon's got his knife into you, and that means you're as good as dead.'

'I know,' Beresford agreed. 'I don't care about any of that. What's getting to me is that the man who hurt Monika will go unpunished.'

'Don't think about that now,' Meadows urged. 'And don't give the bastards the satisfaction of getting rid of you. Hand in your resignation straight away, before they can do anything.'

'And what would I do next?' Beresford wondered. 'I've always been a bobby – it's the only thing I know.'

'I could get you a job as head of security, earning three times as much as you are now,' Meadows said.

'*You* could?'

'Yes.'

'And might I ask how?'

'I know people,' Meadows said.

Yes, Beresford agreed silently – she probably did.

'We could hand in our resignations together,' Crane said. 'How's that for a grand gesture?'

'You're resigning, too?' Beresford asked, amazed.

'My old tutor contacted me a few weeks ago to tell me there's a fellowship in my college available, and if I want it, then it's as good as mine. There's a lot to be said for it, you know. A couple of hours teaching per week, and, for the rest of the time, waited on hand and foot by my scout. It would give me a chance to find out if I really am a serious poet or just a dilettante.'

'What about you, Kate?' Beresford asked. 'Will you stay on in the force if we go?'

Meadows shook her head. 'No, I don't think so.'

'Then what *will* you do?'

'I've never actually *needed* to work since my husband was killed,' Meadows said. 'Maybe I'll become one of the international jet set – summer in St Tropez, winter in Klosters, and the occasional trip to the West Indies or New York for a little bit of variety.'

At any other time, Beresford and Crane would have grasped this opportunity to learn more about Meadows's secret life with both hands, but now it didn't seem to matter.

'We'll be miserable, each and every one of us,' Crane said.

'Yes, we will,' Meadows agreed.

It occurred to them all – practically simultaneously – that the one circumstance they had not factored into their future plans was Monika Paniatowski coming back to work, and that the reason was that, though they knew she *could* come out of her coma at any time, none of them thought she would.

'Phone call for you, Inspector Beresford,' the barman called out. 'Do you want me to transfer to the phone in the corridor, like always?'

'Yes, please,' Beresford said, standing up.

Meadows grabbed his arm. 'If it's some woman offering you a night of hot, uncomplicated sex, take it,' she said.

'I couldn't,' Beresford told her.

'It'll make it easier for us,' Meadows insisted. 'If you've gone, Jack and I can piss off, too.'

Beresford made his way to the corridor, where – between piles of beer crates and the men's toilet – the other pub phone was to be found.

He thought about all the messages that had reached the team via this phone – and of all the cases which had been solved as a result of those messages. But it wasn't going to be like that this time – there was *no way* it could be like that.

'Speak to me,' he said fiercely, into the mouthpiece.

'Meester Colin, is that you?' asked a worried female voice.

'Yes, it's me, Elena. What can I do for you?'

'I have a problem, Meester Colin,' the housekeeper/nanny said. 'Mrs Monika is my boss, but Mrs Monika is not here, and even though I am two years older than my cousin Louisa, I think that she is in charge now.'

'It surely doesn't have to come down to that,' Beresford said, wishing he'd decided to duck this particular phone call. 'Can't you just act as if nobody is the boss, and you're just two girls sharing a house?'

'But it is not right, this thing that she is going to do, Meester Colin, it is not right at all.'

'What's not right?'

'Inviting that boy to stay with us.'

'What boy? Do you mean John Green?'

'Yes.'

'Are you sure you've got that right, Elena?' Beresford said. 'You're certain she didn't just say John would be calling round?'

'She is upstairs making up her mother's bed for him, even while we are talking,' Elena said.

'I'll be right over,' Beresford promised.

Louisa was leaning against the garden gate when Beresford pulled up in front of her house.

'You look like you're waiting for something,' Beresford said.

'I am,' Louisa told him. 'I've been waiting for you. Elena told me she'd called you.'

'Ah!' Beresford said.

'I want John to stay here, and he's going to stay here,' Louisa said. 'And there's nothing you can do about it, Uncle Colin.'

'Would you mind if I came inside for a few minutes?' Beresford said, heading towards the gate.

'Yes, I would mind, as a matter of fact. If I let you inside, you'd only lecture me – and I refuse to be lectured.'

'This boy's just been involved in a very nasty murder case, and two particularly unpleasant suicides,' Beresford reminded her.

'No, he hasn't,' she said. 'He's not been *involved* at all. Through no fault of his own, he was trapped in the middle of them, and like the hero he is, he's come out the other side unscathed.'

He should have sent Crane, Beresford thought. Crane spoke in the same way she did, because he *thought* in the same way she did. He would have known how to handle her.

But it's not Crane's problem, he rebuked himself. It's my responsibility, and I should deal with it.

But how? Louisa had already turned around and was starting to walk back to the house.

'How would your mother feel about this?' he called out desperately. 'Have you thought about that?'

Louisa stopped and turned around. 'As a matter of fact, Mum rather likes John,' she said.

'Pull the other one,' Beresford said harshly. 'I'll bet she's never even met him.'

'Well, no, she hasn't, exactly,' Louisa admitted, 'but the last time she came to school for a parents' evening, I pointed him out to her – and she said he looked rather nice.'

'Is that what you did on parents' evenings – pointed out all the boys so your mother could grade them for you?'

'Why are you being so mean to me?' Louisa asked, her lower lip trembling slightly.

Because I love you, and I don't want you making a mistake, he thought.

'Because not only are you being very stupid, but you're lying to me to cover just how stupid you're being,' he said. 'You didn't point John Green out to your mother at all – you're just saying that.'

'I did point him out,' Louisa said firmly. 'I pointed him out – and nobody else.'

'And why would you do that?'

'Because of Thomas and James.'

'Who?'

'Thomas and James. They're the twins.'

'I know who they are, but I still don't understand . . .'

'Because she's got twins of her own, I thought Mum might be interested to see some older twins.'

'Are you saying that John and Mary were twins?'

'Well, you knew they were in the same class,' Louisa said, 'didn't it ever occur to you that they might be twins?'

No, it hadn't.

'Oh, dear God,' Beresford moaned.

'What's the matter, Uncle Colin?' Louisa asked, sounding slightly worried.

'I want you to do something for me,' Beresford said shakily. 'There are things I need to set in motion, and I can't do that while you're here, so I need you to get into my car right away.'

'This is some kind of trick, isn't it?' Louisa asked.

'It's not a trick,' Beresford said. 'Please, Louisa, trust me on this.'

'It's just a way of stopping me preparing a room for John,' Louisa said. 'Well, I'm not falling for it.'

Beresford moved fast, opening the gate, and grabbing her arm before she knew what was happening.

As he dragged her back down the path towards his car, she dug her heels in.

'If you resist me, I'll handcuff you,' Beresford said.

'Who do you think you are – and just what do you think you're doing?' Louisa screamed at him, as she lost another few inches in their tug of war.

Beresford stopped pulling her, though he did not release his tight grip on her arm.

He looked into her eyes.

'Who do I think I am?' he asked – and there was fury in his voice. 'I'm your mother's best friend. And what do I think I'm doing? I'm trying to save her life!'

EIGHTEEN

He entered the hospital through one of the service doors, just as dusk was falling. Already, only just inside the building, he was encountering a problem he hadn't anticipated – a difficulty he hadn't previously considered – because though he knew how to get to Monika Paniatowski's room from the main entrance (he had cleverly made sure of that the previous day), he had no idea where he was in relation to the room now.

He looked down at the red line, painted on the floor to guide visitors. Where did that connect with the yellow line, which was the one he needed to follow? Did it *ever* connect with the yellow line?

He was tempted to beat a retreat, to come back again the next day, when he was feeling stronger and more resolute, but he knew he simply did not have that luxury – had known it ever since the moment he'd heard the news item on the local radio station.

'*The hospital reports that DCI Paniatowski is showing definite signs of coming out of her coma, and the police expect to be able to talk to her tomorrow,*' the newsreader had said.

And he could not allow that to happen, could he? – especially now he was starting his new life.

He was still standing there, on an empty corridor, with a bunch of flowers in his hand. If any of the staff saw him, and asked him what he was doing there, he might just be able to persuade them that he was a visitor who had got lost. But that wouldn't be good, either, because once Monika Paniatowski's body was discovered, the staff member was bound to remember him, and it was not enough for him to kill Paniatowski – he wanted to get away with it.

The overhead lights flickered, and then went out. For a moment, the corridor was in complete darkness, and then the orange emergency lights came on, generating enough illumination for him to see where he was going, but not much more.

'We are experiencing a temporary loss of power,' said a reassuring voice over the loud speaker system. 'Please keep calm. If you are attempting to reach the post operative recovery wing and can see a green line at your feet, take a left turn and keep walking until you reach the yellow line. If the line at your feet is red, take a right turn and keep walking until you reach the yellow line. If you are attempting to reach the emergency room, and there is a purple line at your feet . . .'

He stopped listening, because now he knew everything that he needed to know.

He silently repeated his instructions, just to make sure he didn't forget them.

Take a right turn and keep walking until you reach the yellow line . . .

Take a right turn and keep walking until you reach the yellow line . . .

The power cut not only meant that he now had directions, he thought, it also offered him the perfect excuse for being lost, though, in these conditions, everyone involved in the hospital would be so distracted that it was unlikely any of them would even take the time to challenge him.

It was almost like divine intervention, he thought.

No, it *was* divine intervention – God was on his side as He had always been on his side.

By the time the full lights came on again – four minutes later – he had managed to find the corridor on which Monika Paniatowski's room was located. Now, his only problem would be if there was someone with her – but looking through the small window, he could see that she was quite alone.

Though he knew he shouldn't, he hesitated.

What would happen if someone came in when he was finishing Paniatowski off? he asked himself.

Then he was doomed, he thought, in answer to his own question – but when it was a choice between certain exposure and possible exposure, it was really no choice at all.

Besides, God would not let it happen – God would keep them all away until he had done what he needed to do.

He stepped into the room, and closed the door behind him.

The last time he'd seen Paniatowski, she had been breathing without any external aid, but now she had a large oxygen mask clamped over the lower half of her face.

He thought it strange that now she was so close to recovery she should need something that she hadn't needed when she was in a deeper coma, but they had said on the radio that her condition had improved dramatically, so he supposed it must have.

He walked over to the bed, and placed his hands around her throat. He did not begin to strangle her immediately, but instead, just stood there, revelling in his feelings of power.

If I squeeze, she dies, he thought, and if I walk away, she lives.

He could understand now why God probably liked being God so much, and – accepting that if you didn't use the power, you didn't really have it at all – he began to squeeze.

What should have happened was that Paniatowski should have started to convulse as she began fighting for air. What actually happened was that Paniatowski's arm suddenly appeared from under the sheet, and her fist slammed – hard – into his nose.

Hardly able to believe what had happened, he staggered back-wards. He had a vague impression that Paniatowski was ripping her mask off, and a second later that she had pulled the top of her head – or at least, her hair – away from the rest of her, and then she was out of the bed, and he could see that she was much slimmer and lighter than Louisa's mum.

'Turn around and put your hands behind your back!' Kate Meadows said. 'Do it now!'

But somehow he was so pained and confused that he was unable to follow her instructions even if he wanted to, and he might have tottered around for some considerable time, had not a kick to the stomach sent him falling backwards in a somersault.

He hit the floor hard, and was still fighting for breath when Meadows turned him over and cuffed his hands behind his back.

'John Green,' Meadows said, 'I am arresting you for the murder of Mary Green, and the attempted murder of Monika Paniatowski. You are not obliged to say anything, but anything you do say may be taken down and used in evidence against you.'

John Green, patched up by the nurse, sat looking across the table in Interview Room B at Crane and Meadows.

'We should have been onto you the moment we started to understand the way the Hidden works,' Meadows said. 'All the children have a nearly perfect attendance record at school, because, that way, they're likely to draw less attention to themselves. Yet when we went to your house on Monday morning, you were there, even though you were clearly not sick. And why were you there? Because you knew we'd be coming. How did you know we'd be coming? You knew because you knew that Mary was dead. And how did you know that – because you'd killed her.'

'I will not deny it, because God does not wish me to,' John Green said.

'The boss tried to warn us about you, as well,' Meadows said. 'She knew that you'd visited her with Louisa.' She paused. 'By the way, it was very clever of you to trick Louisa into showing you where her mother was, so you could find her again when you needed to.'

'I was led by the Lord,' John said.

'Interesting justification,' Meadows said. 'Anyway, as I was saying, the boss tried to warn us. She kept repeating "Loui'a" and "twin". She got very upset about it. We thought she meant the twins – her children – but of course she didn't. "Twin" was you, and she had to call you that, because though she'd seen you in the woods, just after you'd strangled your sister, she didn't know your name.'

'What do you want from me?' John Green asked.

'We'd like you to tell us the whole story. Can you do that?'

'Why not? I first became suspicious of my sister Mary when I saw her using the pay phone in school.'

'Why?'

'Because only the Trusted Ones are ever allowed to use telephones.'

'I see. Carry on.'

'She was calling *him*, of course – that filthy outsider – though I didn't know it at the time. I noticed that she always called at the same time, and I got Jennifer Black to stand near the phone the next time she made a call.'

'Why did Jennifer Black agree to help you?'

'Because she knows that soon I will be a Trusted One.'

'Ah, yes, of course.'

'Jennifer heard enough for me to work out that my sister and this creature were going to Stamford Hall the next Sunday, and I made up my mind, then and there, that I would go there myself.'

'Why?'

'To catch her in the act – to confront her with her betrayal of everything we believe in.'

'How did you get there?'

'I took the shuttle bus, and walked from the main gate to the woods.'

'And did you catch them together?'

'No, as I was approaching the woods, the animal was already driving away on his motorbike.'

'So you went into the woods to look for her?'

'Yes.'

Even from some distance away, he can hear her crying, but her tears fail to melt his heart.

When he finally reaches her, he finds her sitting on the ground, with her head buried in her knees. It is only when he coughs that she looks up.

'What . . . what are you doing here?' she asks.

'I came to catch you in your wickedness,' he says.

'There's been no wickedness,' she tells him.

'Don't lie to me!' he screams. 'You have let that beast – that filthy creature – have his way with you, and now he has slaked his lust, he has abandoned you, like the whore of Babylon you have proved yourself to be.'

'No,' she sobs, 'it's not true. The reason he left me was because I wouldn't do what he wanted.'

But it is obvious to her that John is not really listening.

'Why did you offer your precious fruit to him?' John asks. 'Why didn't you offer it to me?'

His words shock her so much that she stops crying.

'To you?' she says. 'But you're my brother!'

'You must know I love you,' he says. 'You must know I watch you.'

'What do you mean – you watch me?' she asks.

'I've drilled a hole in the wall between my bedroom and yours,' he says. 'I watch you through it. You're even more beautiful than I imagined you to be.'

'And you're sicker than I ever thought anyone could be,' she says.

He falls down on his knees beside her. 'His poison is inside you, but it is not too late for us to purify you,' he says.

'What do you mean?'

'I am God's servant. In three years' time, I will be a Trusted One. Allow me to travel up the same passageway as that beast, and I will cleanse you.'

'I'm still a virgin, and you're my brother,' she screams.

'How can you prefer him to me?' he roars, grabbing her by the throat. 'How can you?'

She tries to fight back, but he keeps on squeezing until there is no life left in her.

'Why did you wash out her vagina with boiling tea?' Meadows asked.

'She still needed to be purified after what she had done with that creature,' John said. 'I intended to cleanse her dead body as I would have cleansed her live one, but I . . . but I . . .'

'But you'd lost your hard-on, and nothing you could do would bring it back,' Crane said.

'It was not my failure,' John Green said. 'The Holy Spirit, which resides in all members of the Hidden—'

'You couldn't get it up – and that enraged you so much that you punished her poor dead body with scalding tea,' Meadows interrupted him.

'I used the tea to purify her,' John Green said calmly.

'She didn't need purifying,' Meadows said. 'When she told you she was a virgin, it was no more than the truth.'

John smiled. 'She was the whore of Babylon, and like all of Satan's agents, you are attempting to deceive me – but it won't work because I have the strength of Almighty God behind me.'

'You saw Monika Paniatowski as you were leaving the woods, you realized that she'd recognized you, and you knew you had to kill her?'

'Yes – I didn't want to, of course, but I had no choice in the matter.'

'No choice?'

'That's right. If I hadn't done anything, I'd have been arrested – and God could not spare me.'

'Well, it looks like he'll have to spare you now,' Crane said.

John Green smiled again. 'Oh ye of little faith,' he said. 'God will rescue me from your wicked hands, just as he rescued Daniel from the lion's den. How do you think I could have found my way to Monika Paniatowski's room, without his help?'

'It seems to me it would be a pretty dumb kind of god who would lead you straight into a trap,' Crane said.

'On this occasion, the devil managed to deceive Him, but the ultimate victory belongs to the Lord,' John Green said.

'It wasn't so much a case of the devil deceiving God as DI Beresford deceiving you,' Meadows said. 'DCI Paniatowski had shown none of the signs of improvement they said she had on the radio – that message was just for you. And it wasn't God who caused the power cut – that was us.'

'But why would you . . .?'

'We'd been following your progress since you entered the hospital, and you'd clearly lost your way. The power cut was the only way we could think of that would put you back on the right track without arousing your suspicions.'

'You're lying, aren't you?' John Green asked.

'You know we're not,' Meadows said.

Green looked at her blankly for a moment, and then he began to bang his head on the table – lightly at first, and then with increasing ferocity.

It took three officers to restrain him until a straitjacket could be found.

DS Higgins stood awkwardly in front of DCI Dixon's desk.

'I've had Barry Hodges released,' Rhino Dixon said.

'So I've heard, sir,' Higgins replied, noncommittally.

'And now, I'd like you to place your warrant card and your handcuffs on my desk,' Dixon said.

'I don't understand, sir,' Higgins protested.

'Of course you do,' Dixon said. 'You're being suspended, prior to an investigation into your conduct during the Mary Green investigation.'

'But you went along with the whole thing, sir,' Higgins whined. 'You said we had a solid case.'

'Yes, I did, didn't I?' Dixon agreed. 'But, you see, I didn't have all the facts then. I didn't know, for example, that though it was DC Bell who discovered Mary's knickers in Barry's room, you'd been in the room yourself for a full ten minutes before Bell began his search. What does that suggest to you?'

'I wanted Bell to search because he had a fresh pair of eyes.'

'You wanted Bell to search because it's always wiser not to discover evidence you've planted yourself.'

'I did it for you, sir,' Higgins said pleadingly. 'I did it to make up for the cock-up when we raided Jim Coles' house.'

Yes, he probably had done it with the best of motives in mind, Dixon conceded, but it had only served to make matters worse.

He could not touch Beresford now – the bastard was probably laughing behind his hand, because though he had initially been wrong about who had killed Mary Green, he had not been all *that* wrong, and anyway, now he had made an arrest, nothing else mattered.

And then there was the press – they would mock him for

arresting the wrong man on top of raiding the wrong house, and
he supposed he couldn't blame them.

The chief constable wouldn't be exactly his biggest fan, either.

And worst of all, he had handed his wife enough ammunition
to torture him unrelentingly for at least a month.

'Sir . . .' Higgins said tentatively.

'The force doesn't need bobbies like you,' Dixon said. 'Put your
handcuffs and warrant card on the desk – and then get out of my
sight.'

EPILOGUE

There had been the first frost of the autumn overnight, and there was still a nip in the air as Louisa, dressed in her smart cadet's uniform, had made her way to the hospital.

Now, she was looking down at her mother, who looked so peaceful that she might just have been asleep.

'I'm loving being a cadet, but it's been a tough first week, Mum,' Louisa said. She smiled. 'Of course, I expect you and all the other old hands would say we're having an easy time of it compared to your day.' She paused. 'The boys are missing you. I've told them that they're such hard work that you needed a holiday from them, but you'll be back soon. And you'd better not prove me a liar – or there will be hell to pay.'

She walked over to the window, and looked out. The trees in the hospital's grounds were starting to lose their leaves, and soon they would be nothing but blackened skeletons.

'What else?' she asked. 'Oh yes, they've made Uncle Colin acting DCI. He didn't want it, but Kate and Jack said that if he didn't agree to keep your seat warm for you, they'd probably bring in someone from outside – and that's the last thing anybody wants.'

She looked down at her watch.

'I have to go, Mum, but I'll call in again later.' She hesitated before speaking again. 'I hope you don't mind, Mum, but I'm using Dad's name at work. It wasn't an easy decision to take, but Police Cadet Louisa Rutter can just be judged on her own merits, whereas Police Cadet Louisa Paniatowski would always be expected to live up to the legend that is her mother.' She examined Paniatowski's face for a reaction, but could see none. 'Anyway, as I said, I have to go,' she concluded.

Paniatowski listened to her footsteps, and heard her close the door with gentle consideration behind her.

Ah, my beautiful, wonderful Louisa, she thought to herself. I wish I could tell you how very, very proud I am of you.

And then, for the first time in a long time, she thought she felt a physical sensation.

It was a tear running down her cheek – she was sure it was.

Or was she?

Maybe it was just her mind playing tricks with her – making her think there was a tear when there was really nothing at all.

But real or imaginary, she chose to take it as a sign of hope.